THE STONE ARBOR

and Other Stories

THE STONE ARBOR

and Other Stories

by

Roger Angell

Short Story Index Reprint Series

BOOKS FOR LIBRARIES PRESS
FREEPORT, NEW YORK

813.54
A583s

STANDARD BOOK NUMBER:
8369-3475-X

LIBRARY OF CONGRESS CATALOG CARD NUMBER:
79-121519

PRINTED IN THE UNITED STATES OF AMERICA

Contents

Castaways

I AM selfish and tired, and vicariousness is what I crave. What I want now is to have a total stranger stop me on the street and say, "I ask nothing of you but to have you listen to my story. I want nothing else from you — not even sympathy. Come into this bar, and I will buy you a drink and tell you about my fascinating life." And then for the next two hours he will talk to me brilliantly, telling me, without interruptions or afterthoughts or sentimentality, a story of many people and places — one that absorbs me entirely. He will be able to let me see the precise expression in his wife's eyes when she looks in a mirror late one evening and decides she is getting older, and, through his words, I will be able to hear the diminishing sound of a distant trolleycar in a small Virginia town thirty years ago. While he talks, he will occasionally have difficulty in suppressing outright laughter, and a few moments later real tears will run out from under his eyeglasses. All the people and events that he talks about will become a part of my life, but then in the end the stranger will shake my hand and we will separate and never meet again. And, for once, I will have had to make no decisions, to offer no kind words or warning or advice. There will have been no demands on me. This is a scene I dream of often.

Do people lean on each other more than they used to, or do all men come to a point in their lives where they find that their true function is to listen to the troubles of those around them and to pretend to be wise and reassuring and full of hope? I come home at night and hang up my overcoat, and my wife comes out of the kitchen and says, "Dan, I wish you'd try to talk to Tony. Something's gone wrong for him, and he won't tell me what it is. He's been up in his room ever since he got back from school." I promise to talk to our son, and then I look through the mail and find a letter from my sister, who lives in Wisconsin. Her two youngest daughters need immediate major dental work, she writes, and her husband (who is an assistant curator in an art museum) has again been passed over for promotion, because the head of his department is suffering from senile jealousy and because my brother-in-law has no social contacts with any of the museum trustees. Although I cannot afford to pay for my nieces' dentistry and cannot understand museum politics, I make a mental note to write my sister in the morning. After dinner, I go up to Tony's room and sit on the edge of his bed and ask him about his schoolwork, and he looks at the floor and blushes and mumbles that everything is fine, and then he starts tearing a piece of notebook paper into tiny squares. Just as I am about to leave, he tells me that his algebra teacher has warned him that he will be dropped from the basketball squad if his marks do not improve, and that his best friend, who visited

us at the beach for a week last summer, has not invited him
to go skiing in New Hampshire during the spring vacation,
although Tony knows he has invited two other classmates.
I sit down again, and start to talk about the algebra. But
there is no way for me to make him like his schoolwork,
and I know that there is no cure for the fears and pains of
youth. Two days later, my wife tells me that someone,
probably the cleaning woman, has stolen fifteen dollars out
of her purse but that she is afraid to accuse her. "It's degrading," she says. She sighs twice, like an overtired child,
and says, "I am degraded. This life is degrading. My fingers
are all cracked from dishwater, and my hair is coming out
in handfuls. We haven't been away alone together for more
than two years. I will not, I simply will not, go back to
Wausaket next summer when we can't afford to join the
Field Club. What are we going to do about it? Oh, how
can you sit there and read and get ready to lie to me about
how everything is going to get better?"

During the weekend, my mother asks me whether elec-
tronic companies are considered a really safe investment,
and whether she should move to a smaller apartment even
though it would mean selling some of the furniture she has
kept from her old house. And at a cocktail party Lynn
Aylmer takes me into a corner and begins to cry. Harry
has started drinking again, she tells me, holding my hand.
"He won't go to a psychiatrist about it," she says. "He
won't talk about it at all. He won't talk about anything.
Couldn't *you* talk to him? Could you have lunch with me
in town someday and tell me what you think I ought to
do?"

I am in the insurance business, and lately it has occurred to me that this may be why everyone I know seems to cry out to me for help. Perhaps there is some spurious professional expression of responsibility and hope that has grown permanent on my face. But how can I explain the impatience I feel these days when I visit a client's office? I sit beside his desk and take out our brochures and rate tables, and he glances at them warily, and then he takes off his glasses and pinches one eyebrow and looks out the window as if he wished he were somewhere else, and then he tells me that he is underinsured and that he must also make plans for more income after his retirement. "But I can't *afford* another big insurance bite," he says. "I've still got two kids to see through college. I've got two mortgages on my house in Scarsdale and a demand note at my bank. I've gone as far in this business as I'm going to get. In another five years, they'll start giving some of my work to a younger man. I'm afraid to take another physical exam." He smiles at me and throws up his hands. "Is there any way you people can help me? There must be lots of other men in my position." He is a pigeon, an absolute pigeon ripe for signing, but what I really want to do is to put my papers back in my briefcase and walk out. Nobody can help him — nobody in this world — and I hate him for being honest and helpless. Even in my office, I'm no longer safe. I know that some afternoon this week George Heller, who works just down the hall from me, will stick his head in my door again and say, "Got a minute, Dan?" George's wife has multiple sclerosis and he has learned to make the best of it, but I will want to shout, "No! Get out of here! Go see your minister, go get drunk. But leave me alone! Stop depending on me." Is it any wonder that I long for vicariousness, that I have started reading murder mysteries, that I want to surround myself with strangers and indulge my new, secret vice of eavesdropping?

About once a month, I get away from home for two or three nights on a short business swing. It shames me to say so, but I have come to look forward to it. Sitting in a dull staff meeting at one of our branch offices, taking an extra Martini before a steak dinner in Locke-Ober's with our New England man, watching a movie alone in the friendly dark — here I am safe, here no one can touch me. I call my wife in the evening from my hotel room, and she tells me that I am missed, and then Tony comes on to say that he has captured a baby squirrel, which he has put in the old hamster cage, and to ask if I will go skating with him on Saturday, and when I hang up, I am struck with a wave of love and longing for them that is warmer and simpler than anything I feel when I am at home. And then, with my feet up on the hotel bedspread, I light a cigarette and look around my neat, empty room, and my heart thumps a little faster as I realize that now I can enjoy the luxury of loneliness, and that I can go out and just look at people and listen to them and be nobody — a fly on the wall, a pair of ears, a free man.

There is a bar off the lobby of the hotel where I stay in Philadelphia that is *made* for eavesdropping. It is small — perhaps twenty tables, close together — and dark enough to make it difficult to read an evening newspaper over one's highball, if one were really trying to read it. There is a serving bar, but no bar proper to encourage lonely conversationalists. Lots of mirrors, set at seated eye level, and the usual bad wallpaper — in this case, silver parrots and cockatoos nestling in black jungle leaves. This bar has been my secret club, my listening post, the den of my little vice. What stories I could tell about the homeward-bound couples who stop there for a nightcap, the late drinkers, and the groups in evening clothes who have clustered in to talk and drink after a party! I know them all; without suspecting it, they have left their indiscreet laughter and their private facial expressions and their dreary and hopeful and impossible confidences with me. It is sad to think that I shall probably never go back there — not after last week, I won't.

I was there last Thursday night. I came in at about ten-thirty and got my favorite table — the small one against the far wall in the middle, next to the round table for six. The bar was about half full; it fills up after eleven. I recognized the couple in the left-hand corner. They are permanent residents in the hotel. He is about sixty, and is a retired small-time judge. Her deepest interest in life is growing roses, and she is profoundly unhappy to be without a garden now that they have sold their big house, which I think was in Villanova. They have one son, who is either in the diplomatic service or else is a career officer in the Navy, and a daughter in Baltimore whose drinking worries them terribly. The judge likes to play the guitar. On this particular night, however, they were out of earshot. I ordered my Scotch and opened my paper, and by remaining absolutely still and concentrating my hearing like a radar saucer I was able to pick up most of a conversation between a couple in their early thirties, who sat directly across from me. They knew each other well. They sat side by side, looking at their Old-Fashioneds and talking slowly. I liked her right away. She had big, serious eyes and long, tapering hands and a way of pausing in the middle of a sentence while she chose the precise words she was looking for. Oh, she was a darling — much too good for the likes of him. He had a blustery way of talking, and over my newspaper I could see that he always smiled when he talked, even though she never looked at him. A charm boy.

"Well," she said at one point, "she probably *isn't* going to die. At least, she's not in a condition where you can expect it right away. At her age, it could be next week or two years from now."

"I know that," he said. "We've both known that for three years. And now she doesn't even know who you are."

"I think she does," the woman said. "At least some of the time. I'm sure she'd know it if there were just a nurse there, or if she was in some kind of a — well, not at home."

"I tell you I *know* all that," he said impatiently, but still smiling. "Those are the facts, so O.K. But I don't see why, on a night when you can't get out, it isn't perfectly all right for me —"

There was a burst of laughter here from a large party at a table near the bar, and I missed what they said next. When I could hear them again, she was saying, in a voice full of tenderness, "— all mixed up playing cards. She drops them and then gets terribly embarrassed, and I even have to look in her hand and make her next play for her."

"All right, damn it," he said. "But why take it out on *me?* You know perfectly well —"

And here I lost them. Four middle-aged women wearing fur coats and carrying concert programs came in and took the table right next to the couple. Their gabble ended my afternoons in that sickroom, where that lovely girl would pour tea for the invalid and draw the blinds at the end of the day and help the old lady sort out her confused and frightening scraps of recollection about gardeners who were long dead and coach dogs who had barked at her when she was a child.

At this moment, I became aware of a voice right next to me — from the big table just to my right. The voice had been there all along, I realized, but I hadn't paid attention, because there were three men at the table, and business talk is apt to be dreary. But this was an unusual voice — deep and confident and pervading. It came from the large man who had his back to me, not three feet away. I picked up his face in the mirror across the room — a big, reddish face with heavy lines running down from the nostrils to the edges of his mouth. He had thick white hair, and his black, curved eyebrows gave him a surprised, almost popeyed expression. The two men with him were much younger; they were both about thirty-five, I'd say, though one of them was almost bald. They hardly spoke at all, and kept their eyes on the large man's face, and I concluded that they were junior employees in his firm. He may not have been their boss, but he was a superior. I could hear every word from their table, and by keeping my eyes on the mirror I could see the expressions and smallest motions of the three of them. It was perfect for me.

"It comes down to a matter of sureness in what you're doing," the big man was saying. "If you're not sure of yourself, nobody will pay one bit of damned attention to you. Don't you agree? Look, George, Martin: you ever trained a dog? You must have. Well, you admit it's got to be him or you. If you're fumbling your way, trying to make a pal of him and train him, too, you'll never get anywhere. Right? Tell you a story. Three years ago, one of our Labradors, Max, started growling at anybody who came by the sidewalk in front of our place. Thought we might have to get rid of him. Well, I'll tell you what I did. I watched him carefully, and the very next time he bared his teeth out there, I took him by the scruff of the neck and dragged him into the garage. I tied him up short with a piece of rope and then got out an old riding crop of mine and beat the absolute living bejesus out of him. He really screamed. Then I put a bowl of water down next to him, keeping him tied up, and I locked the doors on him and kept him in there, in the dark, for twenty-four hours. I told my wife that when I went back we'd either have a ravening, crazy animal who'd have to be destroyed or a good, dependable dog. Cruel, you'd say, wouldn't you, Martin?"

"Well, it *sounds* a little extreme," the bald one said.

"Well, sir, I went back the next morning and let out Max —he jumped up and wagged all over the place, sore as he was — and from that day to this he's been the friendliest, quietest, gentlest dog we have. It worked. It worked because, God damn it, I knew what I was doing, and I had the nerve to act on my knowledge. Let's do this again. Same all around?"

I saw that the two younger men hadn't finished their drinks, but they both downed them quickly and took fresh ones. The big man wasn't really drunk, I decided, but he'd had quite a few.

"I guess it's leadership I'm talking about," the man said after taking a swig from his new highball. "It's an old-fashioned word — an *unstylish* word these days. I think it's going out. That's why I'm talking to you men like this. Good men, both of you. I've been watching you. But by *God*, how do you two plan to get ahead — way ahead — if you go on just doing your work well and being just nice guys? I don't understand people any more. Everybody wants to be liked, and that's all."

"Oh, maybe not as much as all that," George said. He was smiling, looking at his glass. "I — I think a man can be liked and still get ahead. But he shouldn't care about being liked, if you know what —"

"Shouldn't care one damn bit," the older man interrupted. "Leadership. Guts — that's what I'm talking about. Individual guts. Look. Either of you ever row in a shell in college? No? Well, I'll tell you a test of guts. It's in the last half mile of a stiff two-mile race. You want to quit. You want to stop and puke and never lift your arms again. But you don't. You keep on pulling. Oh, maybe it's a little because of the others in the boat and not wanting to let them down. But mostly it's because of *you*. You know it's a test and you know if you quit, you'll never get over it for the rest of your life. You'll never be a leader. Damned if I don't think most men go through life these days without ever testing their courage once. Not even once. They're followers, not leaders."

At this point, the two younger men started talking about the Pennsylvania college crew, trying to get the man off his theme, and I ordered myself another drink. I'd had enough of him. But the couple across the way had left, and I couldn't get away from that voice. I could feel myself leaning toward their table, which is something I try not to do.

"No, I want to get back to our subject here," the man said. "The subject is leadership. Martin, you were in the Army, weren't you? A lieutenant, or some such? Were you ever in combat?"

"A few times," the bald one said.

"Would it surprise you if I said that wasn't the kind of guts or leadership I mean at all? Because the Army's too easy. You take orders and you hand them on. You can't run. You do what you're told. Right? No offense, of course. Nothing personal in what I said, you understand?"

"Sure," said Martin. He'd stopped looking at the man.

"Sure," said the big man. "No, the Army is mass society these days. It's more of getting along with the other fellow. Even the generals don't lead any more; they hold a staff meeting instead. Just like in business firms. No, let's invent an example. Let's take a desert island. Let's say this is a desert island and we've all just been wrecked — the three of us and a few more. It's a rough do. We're going to be here for months. What do we do first, hey?"

"I don't know," George said after a moment. "Look for water. Elect a leader."

"*Ha!*" The big man guffawed so loudly that I jumped, just like the other two. "*Elect* a leader! I'll be God-damned! That's just what you would do, isn't it? And if you were nominated for leader, you wouldn't even vote for yourself, would you?"

George looked up at him in surprise. He was a little flushed. "Maybe not," he said. "It depends."

"I'll bet you wouldn't, George," the older man said. "Because you're a gentleman. You're just another nice guy, George. You're thinking about whether the neighbors will like you. But this isn't an outing with your kids. We're shipwrecked now, remember — you, me, everybody in this room. And it's a question of survival. The right leader may mean the difference between living and dying. The leader — the man with guts and faith in himself — would know it had to be him. He would have to take over. That shocks you, doesn't it, young man? Well, I'll tell you something else. He'd have to take over *even if another man had been elected leader*. There might well be some violence. Yes, there probably would be violence."

There was a moment of silence, and I discovered that I was trembling a little. And then the bald younger man, Martin, spoke, in a tone of voice he hadn't used before. "Yes," he said curtly. "I agree with you. There would be violence."

He sounded so different, so sure of himself, that for a moment I thought he had jumped up and was looking down at the big man. I could see in the mirror that he hadn't, but before I could check myself I swung around and looked right at the three of them. I had never done such a thing before. There I was, an arm's length away from the big man's back; I could see how his suit was stretched by the fat and muscle of his shoulders. The two younger men slowly raised their heads and watched me. I looked at one of them and then at the other. Secretly, almost imperceptibly, George smiled at me, right past the big man's ear, and then, so gently that I nearly didn't see it, Martin nodded to me.

The sweat started out on my palms. I could feel the hot sand of the island beach through my tattered shoes, and the noonday sun burning my arms. Without a second's pause, I silently drew the rusty machete from my belt (it was the one weapon we had saved from the wreck) and grasped it in both hands. I kept my eyes on the place — the little roll of fat on his big neck, just below the hairline — and swung with all my might, like a man swinging a ball bat. There was no noise. He didn't even take a step. Only his arms stiffened, and then he fell heavily on his face in the sand. As he fell, all the silver parrots and cockatoos started out of the black leaves of the jungle trees and flew around our heads, filling the bright air with their ugly cries and the heavy thrashing of their wings.

I never looked back at them. I didn't even finish my drink. I got up from the table and went over to the serving bar and paid my tab, and then I walked out, looking away from their table. I went up to my room and undressed and washed and got into bed. I lay there, smoking a cigarette in the dark, and I thought, Damn him. Damn them. They never said a word to me, but they made me kill for them. We all lean on each other. We depend on each other. We're all stuck on the same island.

The Stone Arbor

AFTER breakfast that morning, old Jason Lowery went down to his cellar to select the wine for the picnic. Although there were only ten or eleven bottles left in the cool, dark place under the stairs, it was almost fifteen minutes before he made his choice. It was harder for him to make decisions these days, and besides, he had been almost certain there were a few bottles left of his own white wine, made from his own grapes. But he could not find them, and finally he settled on two bottles of Piesporter. He came slowly up the stairs, stopped for a moment in the sunny front hall while he caught his breath and checked the labels, and then went outdoors. It was a gilded, brilliant morning, already quite warm — the particular moment in the year when you felt that spring has gone and that you can count on a long succession of unchanging, heat-heavy days. Carrying a bottle in each hand, he walked slowly and carefully down the sloping lawn, passed between the two tall white lilacs his wife had planted, and entered the little woods path that led to the Stone Arbor. It was only fifty or sixty yards long, this shadowy, winding passage through the trees, but

Lowery felt, as always, that it was longer and more important — a path that led to stillness and private delight. And
today the ritual nature of his errand, the expectation of the
party to come, and the familiar weight of the bottles in his
hands made him think for a moment that he was also making a passage into the past.

When he arrived at the clearing in the trees, he went past
the Stone Arbor and the statue, down to the narrow brook.
Here he gently laid the bottles in the cold, moving water,
placing them in a shallow spot where the sun would not fall
on them, with their necks just protruding from the stream.
Farther up the hill, Lowery knew, there was a spot where
the brook broadened into a shallow pool, which was filled
with thick watercress. For a moment, he considered climbing up there, over the steep and tumbled rocks, to pluck a
handful for the picnic salad, just as he had always done in
the past. But then he rejected the idea; it would be too far
for him now and too tiring, even though this would almost
surely be the only picnic of the year. He stood up, straight-
ening the twinge from his back, and lit a cigarette and
walked back to the Stone Arbor. Here, on an impulse, he
began to pull up strands of honeysuckle and ivy from the
ground beside the path. When he had enough, he wound the
tough, trailing tendrils around each other until he had made
a garland, which he placed gently around the neck of the
little stone statue. It had been many years since he last did
this, and now, sitting on one of the wooden benches beside
the arbor, he admired his handiwork, moved by the old
charming effect of the green leaves against the lichened gray
stone of the Roman figure — a naked goddess who held her

slim arms above her head and looked upward, forever smiling at the pagan trees. "The nymph Clymene," Lowery said
gently to himself.

The Stone Arbor was a low fieldstone wall that formed
an irregular, five-sided enclosure, paved with soft, faded
bricks. At each angle in the wall there stood a thick granite
pillar, and on top of these, perhaps twelve feet above the
ground, there were oak beams connecting the pillars and
supporting a crisscrossed network of stringers, made of
peeled saplings. Six grapevines grew here, now so thickly
twisted and interwined that they formed a solid canopy,
cutting off all sunlight inside the arbor save for a few small
patches that danced and shifted on the mossy bricks as the
wind moved the leaves. The open end of the arbor faced the
brook and a small natural platform of stones, on which the
statue stood. Jason Lowery had built the arbor with his own
hands forty years before, in the first summer after he and
his wife bought the house. The statue had been a gift from
his father, given a year later. It had immediately taken its
place as the altar stone, the ritual centerpiece of the large
picnics he and his wife held at the Stone Arbor every summer Sunday. Always those picnics had been talkative, intense
affairs, marked by a scrupulously observed informality, an
innocence fervently and intellectually cultivated. Always
there were painters and sculptors and poets and novelists at
those picnics — people whom Lowery had met and corre-
sponded with in connection with his small job as a three-
day-a-week reader with a New York publishing house.
Sometimes there were neighbors, too — those few who
"understood" — and later there had been children, includ-

ing the Lowerys' own son and daughter, who went barefoot and climbed the pillars and munched sandwiches and scrambled after the frogs in the brook. Padraic Colum had read his poems aloud in the Stone Arbor and so had Robert Frost. Once, somebody had brought Carl Sandburg, who played a guitar and sang songs, and they had even staged a string-quartet concert there on one warm August night, when the arbor was hung with Japanese lanterns and the woods loud with cicadas. Lowery recalled that a thunderstorm had passed close by that evening, and he could still remember how its menacing growls and rumbles had added a further meaning, an overtone of courage, to the thin, exquisite thread of melody from the violins.

But those had been the special occasions; most of the picnics had been indistinguishable from each other — endless pleasant afternoons of talk and laughter and hot discussion, only rarely made memorable by the unexpected arrival of a celebrity or a copperhead. It was an obscure Irish playwright who had finally given a name to the statue. He was a red-headed young man who had worn a striped Basque shirt, white ducks, and leather sandals. Sitting on a bench inside the arbor, with a paper plate of salad on his knees, he had gestured with his fork at the statue. "She's facing toward the west, isn't she?" he had said. "Call her Clymene. You know — the nymph Clymene. The lover of Apollo and the mother of Phaëton, I do believe. Just like this one, she lifted her arms toward the sun and the sky. A charming wench altogether."

What capricious games his memory played, Lowery thought now, puffing on his cigarette. He couldn't even remember that playwright's name or what had ever happened to him, but at this moment he recalled his exact words and could almost hear the faint, charming brogue with which he had pronounced that word "altogether." More and more, lately, he had found this happening to him. Vast congeries of people and names, the titles of books, hundreds of lines of poetry, whole roomfuls of friends, the names of streets in Paris and Boston, faces he had once seen in his office or at college for weeks and months on end, the names of old dogs he had raised and fed and loved, the name of his late wife's sister — all these would vanish suddenly and inexplicably from his mind, to be replaced by arbitrary minor scenes, tones of voice from the nineteen-twenties, chitchat with long-dead grocers, snatches of thirty-year-old weather, the stubborn look on his eight-year-old son's face when he had punished him, so long ago, for defacing the page of a fine book. It was embarrassing, even degrading. Why, just the week before, when he was serving cocktails to the nice young couple from down the hill (*Armitage* — that was *their* name!), he had started to quote to them the quatrain that Elinor Wylie once wrote in a letter to him after she had spent a weekend at the house. It was a bit of verse he had long known by heart, a poem in which she described seeing a unicorn in the woods beside the Stone Arbor. But when he wanted to recite it, it had dropped utterly from his mind. And then he had discovered that he had forgotten Elinor Wylie's name, too. Angry and flushing, he had excused himself momentarily and gone up to his study to find the old letter. (He knew perfectly well where it was — either in the right-hand drawer of his secretary or in the big scrapbook.)

But he hadn't been able to lay his hand on it. He must have stayed up there longer than he realized while he searched for it, lifting papers and taking down books and muttering to himself, for when he came downstairs again, the Armitages had left.

Lowery threw away his cigarette and stood up. He decided he would go back to his study and find that letter now — now, while he remembered it. It might be amusing to bring it out this afternoon and read it to his son. He would wager that Howard had *never* put that verse to memory! But before he went, he had something else to do here, an unpleasant thing — a painful tour of inspection which he forced himself to make almost every day now. He walked around the arbor and clambered up the uneven ground and through the rough shrubbery that rose steeply up from the brook and the clearing. Twenty yards farther on (he was shocked every time at how close it was), the hillside suddenly came to an end; it had vanished, literally overnight — trees, stones, rhododendrons and laurel, poison ivy and rabbit lairs, tons and tons of earth. In its place now there was an enormous gash, a crevasse fifty feet deep and four hundred feet across, cut right through the hill. At its bottom, Lowery could see two immense, smooth paths of dirt that ran north and south, cutting close to the old hickory trees to the west of his house, farther up the hill; curving, in the other direction, close to the village and the schoolhouse and then swinging away toward the river valley and upstate. It was the new highway ("Superhighway!" Lowery said scornfully, repeating the ugly word to himself), almost entirely completed back to the city, thirty-seven miles away, and soon to complete tremedous farther leaps to the north. Today, the raw, unnaturally straight valley was empty; the trucks were parked in neat rows, and the great yellow bulldozers and caterpillars and earth movers stood silent and unmoving. For a moment, Lowery wondered wildly whether the whole project had not been abandoned, whether the legislators and the builders and the planners had not realized their enormous error, and were now only resting before they came back to replace what they had destroyed — to put back the mountains and replant the trees. But then he remembered that this was a holiday, Memorial Day, and he knew they would be back tomorrow. He could even see how much they had done since his last visit here; they were almost ready for the concrete. As he turned and started back, he noticed that the sun had faded, half hidden behind a wan skim of clouds. Even the weather was failing him today. He looked across the little hollow in which the Stone Arbor lay and up to the opposite hillside, where his other property line ran. Soon, he reminded himself angrily, that would be changed, too. Any day now — in a few weeks at most — he would hear the screams of saws again and would come down to find the trees gone, the hillside lowered, and the light let in. After that (to an old man, he knew, it would seem minutes later), he would see the roofs of houses there, whole rows of identical, impossible houses, and the sounds would be let in, too: the clatter of power mowers, the slamming of bathroom doors, the rhythms of washing machines and Detroit hotel dance bands; the noises of sports-cars arriving, doctors and dry cleaners departing, children being summoned, television channels being altered, barbecue parties being organized and consummated; all the ugly, predictable din of domesticity — weeping, gaiety, drunkenness, rages, games, and gossip.

He could not get used to the idea. He *would* not get used to it, by God! They would see! Maybe even tomorrow they would learn. You couldn't just surround a man.

When Lowery got back to the house he let himself in as quietly as possible, holding the screen door behind him and then walking silently across the cool living room and up the stairs to his study. Ever since his wife died, he had avoided the living room when he could; it was too big for him, for one thing, and too neat. Only in his little study did he feel protected now, close to his sets of books, his photographs and letters and water colors — reminders of who he was. And he could close his door; he had an idea that Mrs. Grimes, the housekeeper, was keeping tab on him, watching his comings and goings, perhaps even making reports to somebody about him — to his son, maybe, or Dr. Strauss, or the neighbors. He always locked his desk now.

In the study, he remembered that he had meant to look for something, but he suddenly felt tired, too tired to do anything except sit down in his big leather chair. Good Lord! Eleven o'clock in the morning, Memorial Day morning, and here he was feeling perfectly exhausted. He knew without looking at his watch, or without even lifting his wrist to see whether he had remembered to put on his watch when he dressed that morning, that it was eleven, because at that very moment he heard the slow, gong-like notes of the church bell coming through the trees from the village and breaking softly around the house. Sitting there, he listened carefully until the next sounds came — the tiny blare of distant trumpets and the uneven thumping of drums as the little American Legion band, two miles away, began the straggling parade that would lead from the schoolhouse down to the village green and up to the flagpole. He smiled sleepily and foolishly at the familiarity of it, reassured by the idea of hearing exactly the same sounds again at exactly the same instant in the year. But then he frowned and made himself sit upright. They must not find him asleep when they came! They must not get the idea that he was soft and old and helpless. He stood up and opened the door of the study and walked out onto the landing. "Mrs. Grimes!" he called loudly. "Have my son and his family arrived?"

He heard the swinging door of the kitchen being opened. "No," she said. She sounded bored. "They haven't come yet. It's only just eleven, Mr. Lowery."

"I want to be informed the instant they come. I shall be doing some work in my study and I may not hear them. The moment they arrive — do you understand?"

"Sure. Don't worry, I'll let you know."

Lowery thought he heard something like laughter, but the closing door cut it off. He stood there angrily for a moment, with his hands on the banister, and then went back into the study and closed the door. He sat down, put his head back, and fell instantly into a soft, shallow sleep.

Three weeks before, Jason Lowery had written a letter to his son, Howard, who lived in Riverdale. He had taken the better part of two days to draft and correct the letter, firmly excising any evidences of petulance or self-pity.

I am perfectly aware [he had written, after the first paragraph] that the demands of your own family and business career are all-absorbing to you. Still, I don't mind admitting to you that I have been shocked to discover that you have so little concern for this neighborhood (where you grew up) and this house (which you shall someday inherit) that you have not yet found time to come up and see the effect of the Superhighway. As I wrote you, it precisely skirts our western line and has taken the Stannards' house, the Whyte property, the Kramers', the Abernathys', and many others. Jacob Dufresne lost his barn and a third of his lot, and later sold out and moved to Fort Lauderdale (I understand that Nicole Dufresne is now very ill with a heart affliction). You would scarcely recognize this neighborhood, the old village green, etc. There is a whole row of shops east of the post office now. In any case, we did not lose any of our land, and I think you will find that I have adjusted, reluctantly but realistically, to this monument to efficiency and overpopulation and eight-cylinder culture.

Now, however, there is a new and more pressing matter. A Yonkers man named Kovacs (a "developer" he is called) has recently purchased the entire Closson estate, which was sold by the executors, plus eleven adjoining acres of Eustace James's (the son of Ralph and Margaret). I cannot imagine what possessed the James boy to accede to this plan and cannot, in fact, bring myself to ask him or even speak to him. But you can well imagine what impends — unless action is taken *at once!* This Kovacs proposes to put up some seventy or eighty houses, all alike, plus driveways, sewage system, adjoining stores. Much of this will be all too visible from our east windows, the Stone Arbor, etc. It is an awful thought. It would be the end of it all here. I have made inquiries locally and even to our assemblyman in Albany and find, to my astonishment, that this cannot be stopped legally, even though the school will be impossibly overcrowded, etc. This sort of thing is permitted by our local "zoning," and a number of our village merchants and officials are even pleased by the prospects of greater business! This advantageous factor was pointed out to me in the letter I received from Albany.

By this point, you will have understood the picture and will appreciate the need for instant and efficient steps. You will be glad to know that I have drawn up a plan — quite a sensible one, I believe, for a man of letters, whose business acumen you have always seemed to scorn. It involves the formation of an association, composed of long-term and responsible residents, and the making of an immediate counter-offer to this Mr. Kovacs — one which will provide him with a small profit, and save all our properties and, I might say, our sanity. Now, Howard, you must realize that I cannot go forward from this point without your assistance. I need your strong arm — your youth, your energy and business knowledge, and, of course, your financial support. (You know the modest nature of my remaining capital.) But I do not hesitate to call upon you, because this is your house, too. It is where your mother lived, and the one place she loved. It will be yours (with your sister), all too soon. Fortunately, due to your ambition and undoubted success, you stand in a position to help us — your family and your old neighbors. Your roof-tree is threatened, Howard. (I may encourage you by reporting that I have held preliminary discussions of these plans with some of our old friends here. They are cautious but deeply interested. All that is required now is a leader, and the Lowerys have been, I might venture to guess, the intellectual and perhaps the spiritual leaders here. We are the guardians of the past, Howard, and the past, believe me, is worth preserving.)

I shall write the substance of this letter to your sister, but she is in no position to help. Please call me or write *at once* and tell me when you plan to come up here. I shall look forward to seeing Eliza and the children as always. My health is excellent, for a man of seventy-one.

Affectionately and hopefully,
FATHER

Lowery received the first answer to his letters from his daughter, Ariel. She was the younger child, a woman of thirty-four now. She had been married three times, most recently to an Austrian ski instructor in Kitzbühel. Her only child, a boy of ten, was living with her first husband in Lake Forest. Lowery had written to her in Mexico City, where she had gone to divorce the Austrian, but her answering letter had come from Acapulco.

How too, too sad about the old place, Daddy [she had written]. I could weep, really. I do so hope Howard will rally around and apply his Merrill-Lynch authorety and $$$. Poor Daddy!

Your letter caught up with me during the *wildest* adventures. Sven and I had come here while he took a job with a travel bureau. Just temporary because nobody is buying sculpture right now. (I wrote you about Sven, didn't I?) Well, two nights ago there was this *incredible* meelee (sp.?) with the local gendarmes. All a fantastic misunderstanding, too complicated to relate. They are just peasants, of course. But one of them got this broken jaw and it is a question of fifty dollars right away or else Sven goes to *jail!* Imagine. So if you could oblige yr. youngest and fondest chick I would be forever your slave. If you could wire it it would be even better. Or maybe you could put it to Howard somehow, useing your famous tact. (Please don't *worry* about this Daddy. I'm alright, truly.)

Let me know about the old house and all love,

ARIEL

Lowery had kept this letter for two days, reading and re-reading it with puzzlement and anger. Finally, he had mailed it to his son, with an accompanying note: "I don't understand this, Howard. Could you look into the matter, perhaps through your office? When are you coming to see me?

The matter is more and more pressing." Two days later, his son's secretary had telephoned from the city to tell him that Howard and his wife would be up on Memorial Day.

It was much darker in the study when Jason Lowery awoke from his nap, and he could hear a gentle drizzle of rain against the windowpanes. He sat there for a moment, weak and sleep-fuddled, listening to the dripping of leaky gutters. There would be no picnic, no Stone Arbor, this day. He stood up abruptly and hurried to the window. They had come! A shiny new sedan stood in the driveway below, its black roof gleaming in the rain. They had come and nobody had awakened him. Maybe they had peered in and watched him sleeping, with his hands limp and his lips open! He was about to turn away from the window when he saw his son beneath him. He was wearing a white raincoat and a tweed cap, and he was peering closely at the corner of the house, beside the peony bed. While Lowery watched, Howard bent down and ran his fingers carefully along the sill of the house, under the clapboarding. The sight of his son examining the house, with his thick neck showing under the silly cap and his foreshortened shoulders looking, from here, enormous, enraged Lowery. What did he think he was doing? He was on the point of throwing up the window and shouting down at him, ordering him out of his flowerbeds, when he paused, trembling. No — that wouldn't do at all. He needed Howard now. He must be firm, businesslike, affectionate. He hurried into the bathroom, where he washed, combed down his short white hair, buttoned the collar of his flannel shirt, and tightened his necktie. He knew what Howard would say first ("Fifty-five minutes from our door to here. That new road certainly makes it easy, far as it goes"), and he resolved not to show his annoyance. He straightened his shoulders, began to smile, and started down the stairs. After all, he reassured himself, Howard was his own son.

Howard mixed Martinis before lunch, and Lowery, anxious to make a pleasant occasion of it, took two cocktails. Howard's wife, Eliza, looking pretty and citified and formal in a white straw hat, did most of the talking at the table. She explained why the children had not come; young Howard was still off at school and Ginny was visiting college friends in Red Bank over the long weekend. Lowery unexpectedly remembered the Elinor Wylie poem about the unicorn, and he recited it quickly. "It's a precise and beautiful thing," he said at the end, removing a bit of salad that had fallen into his lap. "It's a — a prayer for this house and what it has been."

After lunch, he hurried into the kitchen to tell Mrs. Grimes to serve the coffee in the Sèvres cups, and he poured out little glasses of cognac to go with it. He was pleased at remembering the poem, and he felt suddenly and happily certain that Howard and Eliza had been softened and touched by their return to this house. And he wanted to show that he could still offer, with fine china and a distinguished liqueur, some evidence of the delicacy and grace that had always been found here. But then, sitting in the high-ceilinged living room with them while the rain beat down outside the long windows, he was stricken by a giddy, terrible wave of new sleepiness. All that liquor had been a serious mistake. Then he noticed his son looking bitterly and petulantly at the delicate coffee cup held in his hand, as if he had discovered such an unlikely object in the house of a bank thief or a garageman. By God, Lowery thought. By God, in a minute he'll ask me how much it cost! He gathered his courage, forced himself to smile again, and rubbed his hands together briskly. "Well!" he said cheerfully. "To business!"

While Lowery talked, Howard walked impatiently around the room. Back and forth he went, twitching at the curtains, lifting ashtrays and figurines, kicking at the carpet corner. Once, Lowery saw Eliza tug at the bottom of his jacket and nod her head toward the sofa. But Howard jerked away angrily and continued his pacing. Lowery talked faster and faster, his hands clenched on his knees. "And as I told you," he said, "it must be done *now*. Kovacs will start cutting trees in a week's time. After that, there'll be nothing left to save. I've talked to Clifford Funk and the others, and it's my belief, almost my conviction, that they're simply waiting to follow our lead. Clifford said —"

"All right, Daddy," Howard said at last, throwing himself down in an armchair. "All right, now. Let's face a few things. Where's Clifford Funk going to get any money for this association of yours? When's he ever had a dollar's worth of change to rub together in his pocket? He's retired, isn't he? He's just living on his pension, isn't he? You've seen his house — how long do you think it's been since it had a decent coat of paint? What's he going to put up — twenty-five dollars? The same for the rest of them. No, Daddy, no!"

He held his hand up as his father started to speak. "Let me ask you something else, Daddy. Have you any idea how much land around here costs? Do you know what Kovacs must have put up to take over forty-four prime acres? Do you know what he expects to clear out of this operation? Where are you going to get that kind of money — from me? Don't make me laugh. I may be doing all right, but I'm not in that league — no sir. And I have a family, too. Don't forget that little factor."

"I *haven't* forgotten," Lowery said firmly. "This house is for them, too. It belongs, in effect, to the entire Lowery family. And I still have some funds. I propose to put up what I can. I don't really think you've looked into the situation as thoroughly as I have."

"You think so, Daddy? You think that?" Howard laughed briefly and lit a cigarette. "Well, I'll tell you one thing. At least I've *talked* to Jerry Kovacs. I went up to see him and have a talk with him." (Lowery's heart gave a great leap of excitement: Howard had already talked to Kovacs! Maybe he had solved the whole matter already! Howard was a businessman — he was paid, well paid, for exactly this sort of thing.)

But his son was still talking. "I'll tell you one thing I found out, Daddy. Jerry Kovacs made you an offer for this place, didn't he? A good cash offer. And you never even answered his letter, did you? Why didn't you tell me about that in your letter?"

Lowery tried to concentrate on the question. (He was really terribly sleepy.) Had that actually happened? "I forgot," he said helplessly. He was telling the truth; he had honestly forgotten all about that letter. He had thrown it away after reading it once.

"I'll bet you did," his son said. "I'll just bet you forgot!"

"You are not to talk to me like that!" Lowery shouted, jumping up. "You are not to talk to your father in that tone of voice! I forbid it! I forbid it! Where is your feeling? Where is your affection for this house and for me and for your mother? Where is your respect?"

Howard was standing, too, and for a moment the two men stared at each other in disbelief and shame. Then Howard turned away and walked rapidly to the window. "Respect!" he said quickly and quietly as he stared out at the rain. "Respect, is it? You forget a lot, Daddy. Sometimes I think you forget awfully easily. But *I* don't. I don't forget the kind of schools I went to. I don't forget sweating my way through college on a scholarship and picking up dirty dishes and delivering newspapers and watching the other ones, the lucky ones, the ones who weren't scared all the time like me. I remember the day I came back from a summer job in the lock factory and found you serving wine to a refugee — some potter or something. Why do you think I work so hard, Daddy? Do you think business is all that much fun? It's just that *my* children aren't going to have that — all that culture and that charm and those debts and the money going. My own mother had to start selling antiques at the age of fifty-five! Have you forgotten that, Daddy? We've all held you up, all of us, when your little job ran out and you took to your precious study upstairs."

He turned to face his father, who had sat down again and was staring at his hands. "What about Ariel, then?" Howard went on. "What about my own sister, your daughter. Take a look at her, Daddy. You couldn't be bothered with her, either, could you? I don't know what was missing in this crazy house to make her like that. I don't know what crazy kind of thing she's looking for all over the world. Maybe she wasn't bright enough for you. Maybe you didn't like her enough. Maybe she disappointed you, the way I did. But take a good look at her now, Daddy! She's just a marrier. She's a plain tramp, sleeping with every Mexican and Swede that comes along."

"Howard!" Eliza cried. "We don't have to have that sort of thing. That doesn't do any good."

"O.K., O.K., I'm sorry." Howard sat down and lit another cigarette, and there was a little silence in the room.

Lowery continued to stare at his hands while he desperately tried to collect his thoughts, to make sentences, to wrestle his mind away from the teetering edge of drunkenness and sleep. It wasn't fair, he said to himself again and again. How could Howard think those things about him? How could he say such things? He felt a wave of self-pity sweep over him at the hand he had been given to play. It was a cliché, a melodrama — an old man fighting for his homestead. Why, it was laughable, really! But there were other things to be said now — things to be said clearly and quickly, if only he could remember them. Mostly, they were things about this house. Because his son simply did not understand. Certainly he had failed in his job. And he had failed in another, more important way, which Howard had never known about: he had not been a doer, a creator. He had not written a book or painted on an easel. His poems, he had learned long ago, were unimportant. More than anything, he mourned that failure. But he had created this house! This place, with its study, its trees, its Stone Arbor, had been, in a sense, his livelihood. And the weekends and the picnics and the talk and the friends had been his act of the imagination — his and his wife's. The others, the visitors, had seen this and had accepted him. Loved him, if you please. But how could he say this? Howard and Eliza couldn't even recognize their names. Suddenly angry, he ran his fingers through his hair and shouted, "We don't all choose to travel at seventy miles an hour, you know!"

He saw Howard and Eliza exchange a quick look, and then Howard leaned forward and began to talk in a new, wheedling tone. "Listen, Daddy," he said. "We don't need to fight. We're different, you and I. I know that. I accept that. I know I've never found favor in your eyes, and maybe it's as much my fault. But I can't help you now. Before God, I can't. It's a dream, that's all. But now listen to this. I told you I talked to Kovacs. He told me that offer is still open. He'll make the exact same offer for this house and property, and I, for one, think it's damned generous of him. You've just got to take it, Daddy. It wouldn't be worth your while, even if you wanted to stay. Before you came down, I took a walk around this place. Why, the whole northwest corner of the house is like paper. It's all rotted in there — sills, uprights, and all. I don't know what it is — termites or dry rot or what. But how are you going to fix that, Daddy? How are you going to pay for something like that? I even walked down to the Stone Arbor, and that's going, too. It smells of rot. You can't really ask me to put my money into a place like this, can you?"

Eliza leaned forward and smiled at him. "You could live down near us, Father Lowery," she said. "We could find you a lovely little apartment. Or a place in the city. The children would love to have you so near."

"Sell out, Daddy," Howard said softly. "It'll give you a fine piece of capital. You'll be fixed for life."

Lowery leaped to his feet. He had to get out of here. He started for the stairs up to the study, and then turned toward the front door. There was a moment in the hall, a giddy moment of too many doors and destinations and decisions, when he thought he would surely fall. But he turned back to face them. "I do not understand you!" he cried out, the tears springing to his eyes. "I do not understand you! You will leave me nothing. You are destroying the past — your builders, your road people, all of you. Why should not old men be mad?"

He stopped — amazed, delighted, even at this moment, by the aptness of the words that had sprung to his lips. He looked at them slyly, at the two plump, puzzled faces. "D'you know Yeats?" he asked. "Have you ever heard of him?

> Why should not old men be mad?
> Some have known a likely lad
> That had a sound fly-fisher's wrist
> Turn to a drunken journalist;
> A girl that knew all Dante once
> Live to bear children to a dunce —

Don't stare at each other! Of course you don't know it. You know nothing! You cannot read. You will grow old. You will grow old, too, and *you* will have nothing to remember — no grace, no beauty, nothing of the past!"

He started for the door, and then stopped again and blew his nose and came back. "Excuse me for a moment," he said with dignity. "I am simply going down to the brook to get my wine. I just remembered it."

Outdoors, the rain had turned to a fine, chilly mist. The cool air brought the tears back to Lowery's eyes, and he walked unsteadily down the garden, his brain whirling with rage, exhaustion, scraps of poetry. "Cuchulain . . ." he whispered to himself. "Crazy Jane . . .

> A King had some beautiful cousins,
> But where are they gone?"

He stumbled over a root and almost went sprawling, and then continued down the path.

> "Battered to death in a cellar,
> And he stuck to his throne . . ."

At the brook, one of his feet slipped while he was recovering the wine, and icy water ran into his shoe. Carrying the cold bottles, he came back to the Stone Arbor and set them carefully down on the path. He went up to the statue of Clymene and started to rip the vines off her neck. They were tougher than he thought, and for a moment before they broke, the statue teetered under the violence of his tugging. He looked at the smiling, unchanging face for an instant and then put both his hands behind her neck and yanked the statue forward off the stone platform and onto the rocks. One of the arms broke off and the head rolled away somewhere. He picked up the bottles and held them before his face. One of the labels had washed off in the water. Lowery shrugged. He hurried around the arbor and again struggled up the scraggly hillside that led to the rock cut. The great pit was filled with mud and shadows, and the machines at the bottom looked like monstrous sea animals, busy over some slow, obscene ritual.

"Go away!" Lowery whispered violently. "Go away!" Then he threw the bottles of wine down there, heaving them, one after the other, as far as he could into the gulf and then listening for the crash of glass below. He took out his handkerchief and wiped his wet hands and dried his face. But before he started back to the house, he peered sharply about him, making one last, hopeless search among the trees for the animal he had so often almost suprised here — the poet's creature, with its sweetly dappled skin, its small, restless feet, and the light of the late-afternoon mist shining from the convolutions of its single, delicate horn.

Some Pigs in Sailor Suits

GEORGE SWAN came out of the revolving door and walked up the three steps to the lobby. He found himself taking off his hat and then wondering why he had. Going into his college club always made him feel that way; it was like walking into the home of a very rich man. Of course, the club had been built that way; the big leather chairs and heavy drapes would never have to be changed. They would be as much in style ten years from now as they were today, or as they had been fifteen years ago, when Swan had first seen the place. He had never joined the club. When he had graduated and come to work in the city, he couldn't afford it, and later, when he could have afforded it, he discovered that there were very few of his college friends who were, like himself, in the cotton-brokerage business. He liked his old friends but no longer could find much to talk to them about, and he and his wife agreed that it would be a waste for him to join. But he liked going back when someone invited him, if only because the club was the one place in the city that never seemed to change.

At the desk, the attendant told him that Mr. Connors was

waiting for him in the bar and he was to go right in. He had started down the hall with his hat in his hand when the attendant called him back to check his hat and briefcase and topcoat at the coatroom by the desk.

In the paneled bar, Swan saw Russell Connors sitting at a round table in a corner with an Army colonel. Connors hadn't changed, either. Swan had seen that the day before, when he had bumped into him on the street and they had made this date for a drink. He was still as thin and red-cheeked as the last time Swan had seen him, five years before. Connors was an executive on a news magazine. Perhaps that was why Swan had agreed to meet him; magazine people were still a little exciting to him. Today Connors was wearing an expensive gray pin-striped suit with a discharge button in the lapel. Swan was a little surprised at the button, for in this spring of 1946 discharge buttons were already beginning to go out of style, possibly because they were the mark of a job-hunter. But nobody would mistake Connors for a man without a job. His shirt collar had rounded points and was pinned under his tie with a gold clasp. His hair was thick and cleanly parted. When he rose and held out his hand, Swan noticed that he wore heavy gold cuff links.

"Hello, Georgie," Connors said, smiling. He shook Swan's hand vigorously. "This is great, simply great. I hope you don't mind my making this party for three. Jim Lovering here was with me in Washington for a while, and he's just back from Japan and all over the map with a lot of interesting dope. Jim, this is Georgie Swan. We were in college together."

"How do you do," said Swan.

"Glad to know you, George," the Colonel said loudly, shaking his hand. "Any friend of Russ's."

Swan sat down, and Connors beckoned to a waiter. Swan saw that the two men were drinking highballs and ordered the same. He looked at the Colonel. Lovering was tanned and looked young, despite his short gray hair. He had a long nose and flaring nostrils. When he lit a cigarette, Swan let his eyes drop to the wings and the three rows of ribbons over his breast pocket. He didn't recognize any of the decorations.

"Jim has been trying to tell me that I got out of the Air Corps too soon," Connors said, grinning. "He thinks I should have turned into a career man and kept my membership card in the Pentagon Commandos."

"Not at all, Russ," Colonel Lovering said. "I knew none of you PRO boys would stick — no reason for it. You're still in the same line and getting more for it now. Only right. I was just saying that this is the real time now. More doing today than any time I can remember. These next five years will see the biggest change in Air Corps history. Vital times, vital times. And I wouldn't miss a minute of it."

"Jim was just telling me about the bomb damage in Japan, George," Connors said. "I know you'll be interested, even if it isn't right up your alley. I'm not all filled in on it myself."

"Certainly," Swan said. "Go right ahead. I'd like to hear about it." He picked up the drink the waiter had brought and looked over the rim of the glass at the Colonel.

"Well," Lovering said thoughtfully, tapping his cigarette in an ashtray, "I had to tell Russ that this is mostly all off the record. The full report isn't out yet, and I can't even tell you

all *I* know. Not yet. But I'll just have to ask you not to re-
peat this around. I know you're not a journalist, but you
know how it is."

"Oh, certainly," Swan said. "Of course."

The Colonel took two swallows from his glass and quickly
put it back on the table. "I was telling Russ about the difference between Japan and the ETO in this business of bomb-
damage appraisal. During the war, that is. Those boys in
England got all hopped up back in '43 and '44 and overesti-
mated their bomb damage. Partly their fault, partly PRO's
fault. Made good reading. Then came the payoff. You remember what happened last spring, Russ."

"Don't I just!" Connors said, shaking his head. "There
was a hell of a stink, even in Washington."

"Sure," the Colonel said. "Natural thing. Those ground-
forces boys got into Germany and they began to look
around. They'd find a target that had been declared wiped
out still producing. Not much, maybe, but still turning out
steel or oil or what have you. And didn't they yell about it.
Y'see, they'd been waiting years for that, just to give the fly
boys the business, and they sure poured it on. We heard
about it right off, out where we were, on Guam. A lot of the
boys with us were from the ETO, and we got smart and real
careful in a hurry. Now we knew, for instance, that the 29s
were raising hell, absolute hell, in Japan. But did we yell
about it? No, sir. We went good and easy . . ."

He was silent as the waiter brought three fresh drinks to
the table. Swan discovered that he hadn't finished his. He
gulped it and handed the empty glass to the waiter. As the
Colonel went on talking, Swan stole a glance at Connors. He

was completely absorbed, looking at Lovering's face. Now and then he would nod his head or smile slightly at something Lovering said. Even when he drank, he never took his eyes off the Colonel.

"And Osaka was almost as bad as Kobe," Lovering was saying. "Wasn't much to choose between any of 'em. And every place the same thing happened. We had to revise our figures upward. Now, in Osaka, we'd figured, still goin' easy, on ten square miles burnt out from photos. That's about twenty per cent of the city. But when we got there, it was a good thirty-five per cent — thirty-five per cent, easy. Why, the Japs themselves estimated over fifty per cent, but of course they'd had a lot of personnel losses and they were still a little excited. Thirty-five per cent is closer. But you can bet that it made us all happy, especially the fly boys."

"And that campaign took fewer bombers than anything in the ETO," Connors said.

"Sure, but it's not the same thing. Not the same at all. I've always been the first to say it. There never was a good test of all-out bombing against a modern city. Over there in Germany they just had GPs and the old incendiaries. That's what they worked with just about all the time."

"GPs?" repeated Swan.

"General-purpose bombs," Connors said to him quickly. "High explosive. Go ahead, Jim."

The Colonel finished his drink. "Now, as you know," he said, lighting another cigarette, "we were dealing almost exclusively with M-69s. Fire bombs were right for Japan.

Those flimsy houses and slums were all built for us. They were what gave us our percentages. And I'm the first to admit that against German cities or any really modern target we wouldn't have looked so good. Now, I look at it like this. In the ETO they had GPs. We had the M-69. But if we'd used the GPs first, say against a big modern city like Chicago, and *then* had come in with M-69s, we'd have had a test. That would have been the real business: GPs to get the walls and concrete, then the fire to burn out the wreckage. Now, that never happened to a city, so we can't tell. But I claim it would be something to see. Yes, sir, something to see." He slapped the table lightly with the ends of his fingers and sat back in his chair, looking from Connors to Swan.

Connors leaned forward toward Lovering. "But doesn't this atomic deal put that all out of date?" he asked in a low voice.

Again the Colonel paused while the waiter served the drinks. This time Swan had finished his, and he picked up a full glass immediately.

"Naturally, Russ," Lovering said. "At least, that's what we all suspect. And we're going to find out more in July at the Crossroads unless these god-damned agitators put a crimp in it. Now, I shouldn't be telling you this" — he glanced quickly over his shoulder and then bent forward across the table — "but I think I've got a good chance to go along on this Crossroads business. In fact, I'll know on Monday. My old boss is in it up to his teeth, and I have a hunch he'll take me on out to Bikini. I want to get in on this Big A stuff. Why, in five years it may be the whole show."

"The Big A?" asked Connors.

"Yeah, that's what I call it," Lovering said.

"Jim, that's damned good," said Connors. "Damned good. The Big A. I like that. Would it be O.K. with you if we used that? It's a new touch — just what we like." He had taken a gold pencil and a little leather notebook from his inside coat pocket.

"Why, sure thing, Russ," Lovering said, smiling. "I didn't think anything about it. It's just what some of the boys call it. Do you really think you'll use it?"

"The Scarlet Letter," Swan said unexpectedly.

There was a pause as the other two men looked at him. "What?" asked the Colonel finally.

"The Scarlet Letter," Swan repeated. "The Scarlet Letter was a Big A."

"What is this, some gag?" asked the Colonel, smiling. "Something from college?"

"That's right," Connors said quickly, looking at Swan. "Just something from college." Swan thought he saw Connors frown at him and shake his head slightly as he put his pencil away. Swan's tongue felt dry. He looked at his glass and then took a big swallow of liquor.

"I just spent two weeks in New Mexico with those kids," he heard Lovering say, "and I've never seen anything like it. Those boy are fighting for the privilege of flying that plane with the bomb just like kids fighting to make the first team in college. It does your heart good. That's what I mean about vital times. I can't remember ever seeing morale so high. Now, you hear all these officers bitching about losing a big army. Not me. I say let's lose 'em. Let's separate the men from the boys. Get the grousers and the malcontents back to their wives, if that's what they want so damned much. We don't want 'em. Let the people who are scared of the future go back home and wait for it to hit them. I'll just stick with those men I saw in New Mexico. They're making the future and they know it. They're happy about it."

"What about those people on Bikini?" Swan asked. "How's their morale?"

"Who, the scientists?"

"No, the natives. I saw a picture of them getting ready to move, and they didn't look so happy."

"Oh, hell," Lovering said in a relieved tone. "You mean the gooks. Well, I wouldn't worry about them. I've seen them, millions of them, and I've seen their islands. Why, the Marshalls are just crawling with lousy islands like that, all alike. Those gooks are just being taken off one and put on another. It'll give them something to talk about and in six weeks they'll forget all about it. Don't worry about the gooks; they're not worried. I'll tell you who *is* jumpy, though. I'll tell you the really nervous boys." He was grinning now. "That's the Navy. Those little boys in blue are just scared breathless they're going to be out of jobs. They're busy as a cat on a tin roof, trying to scratch up some excuse for themselves if this test does what we think it will to their ships. Christ, I have to laugh. After the way those boys carried on about winning the war out there singlehanded."

"I understand they're going to dress the pigs in sailor

suits," said Swan. He put his empty glass down on the table, conscious of the eyes of the other two men on him.

"What?" said Connors.

"In the test — that test," Swan said, looking at the table. "All those pigs. I read about it."

"Oh," said Lovering, "I know what he means. You mean flashproof clothing, like the sailors wear, don't you?" he asked loudly, as if Swan were deaf.

"And goats in the turrets," Swan said. He was feeling a little drunk, and he tried to concentrate on Lovering's face. "Go ahead," he said. "Tell about those pigs."

"Well, you're right about those pigs and goats," Lovering said as Connors waved to the waiter again. "The medics and the scientists want wounded animals, not dead ones. They want to test victims. They got pigs and goats because they're big, like men. And pigs have a skin like human skin. Some of the pigs will wear flashproof clothing, like Navy gunners. They've got rats, too — thousands of 'em. I don't know too much about that, though — not my line. This show is more for the medics and the Navy. Now, if they were testing a city, I'd have been in on it from the start. That's one thing that was too bad about Hiroshima and Nagasaki. With the war still on, we couldn't do much but drop the things. A war's a bad place for a really scientific test. Can't get in quick enough to check on immediate results. Photos, sure, but what can you tell from photos? By the time you get in, the casualties are gone, personnel replaced, streets policed up. Nothing to do but look at what's left and make a guess at your effectiveness. No, I say the Big A was never really tested against a city — scientifically tested. And, as I said, those Jap cities are no real criterion. I saw 'em — I know."

"That's true, Jim, very true," Connors said. "I'd never realized that, but I'm sure you're right."

"No doubt about it," Lovering said, picking up the fresh drink the waiter had just brought.

"Now, Jim," Connors began, leaning forward, "this is presumptuous and don't feel that you have to answer. But just what do you believe would happen in a big city like this? Off the record, of course."

"Well, now," the Colonel said, and then paused. "Well, I think that's a fair question, Russ. Something I've been considering, too. Matter of fact, I looked at the city with that in mind yesterday in the taxi when I came from the station. But even with this old Model T bomb they're using at Crossroads it's hard to say. You have lots of imponderables, new factors: skyscrapers, subways, all permanent buildings, and the like. But I think these civilian extremists are way off in one thing, and that's blast damage. From all I know, it would be much less, with this old bomb, than they estimate. Sure, you'd lose walls, plenty of small buildings in residential districts, but all replaceable stuff. Maybe a few big buildings, but not half what they figure. Of course, your big losses would be from the heat — personnel losses."

"What?" said Swan.

"I say it's the heat that'll be most effective, not blast," Lovering said. "So your main losses would be personnel, not construction."

"You mean people?" Swan asked in a loud, angry voice.

"Yeah," said the Colonel, puzzled. "People — personnel.

Nothing irreplaceable. Depend mostly on the time of day for your casualty figures, of course. But your permanent features — buildings, streets — would take it better than most people imagine."

"You've got it down pretty fine, haven't you?" Swan said after a moment. "I'll bet you know the percentages already, don't you? They're all right in your head."

"How do you mean?" asked the Colonel. "I don't get you. As I said, it's just my estimate. We don't know for sure. We're just working with pigs and battleships now. Not cities. Does that answer your question?"

But Swan, looking angrily at the Colonel, didn't reply. Finally, it was Connors who spoke. He was looking up at the high ceiling of the paneled bar, his drink held neatly away from his crossed legs and well-pressed trousers. "It would be something to see, though, wouldn't it?" he said musingly. "A big place like this, I mean. A whole city, all built up like this."

"Hell, yes," said the Colonel, smiling. "It'll be something to see, all right."

Tennis

THE thing you ought to know about my father is that he plays a lovely game of tennis. Or rather, he used to, up to last year, when all of a sudden he had to give the game up for good. But even last summer, when he was fifty-nine years of age, his game was something to see. He wasn't playing any of your middle-aged tennis, even then. None of that cute stuff, with lots of cuts and drop shots and getting everything back, that most older men play when they're beginning to carry a little fat and don't like to run so much. That wasn't for him. He still played all or nothing — the big game with a hard serve and coming right in behind it to the net. Lots of running in that kind of game, but he could still do it. Of course, he had slowed up and he'd begun to make more errors in the last few years and that would annoy the hell out of him. But still he wouldn't change — not him. At that, his game was something to see when he was on. Everybody talked about it. There was always quite a little crowd around his court on the weekends, and when he and the other men would come off the court after a set of doubles, the wives would see their husbands all red and puffing. And then they'd look at my old man and see him grinning and not even breathing hard after *he'd* been doing all the running back after the lobs and putting away those overheads, and one of them would say to him, "Honestly, Hugh, I just don't see how you do it, not at your age. It's *amazing!* I'm going to take my Steve off cigarettes and put him on a diet. He's ten years younger and just look at him." Then my old man would light up a cigarette and smile and shake his head and say, "Well, you know how it is. I just play a lot." And then a minute later he'd look around at everybody lying on the lawn there in the sun and pick out me or one of the other younger fellows and say, "Feel like a set of singles?"

If you know north Jersey at all, chances are you know my father. He's Hugh Minot — the Montclair one, not the fellow out in New Brunswick. Just about the biggest realty man in the whole section, I guess. He and my mother have this place in Montclair, thirty-five acres, with a swimming pool and a big vegetable garden and this En-Tout-Cas court. Almost an estate. My father got a little name for himself playing football at Rutgers, and that helped him when he went into business, I guess. He never played tennis in college, but after getting out he wanted something to sort of fill in for the football — something he could do well, or do better than the next man. You know how people are. So he took the game up. Of course, I was too little to remember his tennis game when he was still young, but friends of his have told me that it was really hot. He picked the game up like nothing at all, and a couple of pros told him if he'd only started earlier he might have gotten up there in the big time — maybe even with a national ranking, like No. 18 or so. Anyhow, he kept playing and I guess in the last twenty years there hasn't been a season where he missed more than a couple of weekends of tennis in the summer-time. A few years back, he even joined one of these fancy clubs in New York with indoor courts, and he'd take a couple of days off from work and go in there just so that he could play in the wintertime. Once, I remember, he played doubles in there with Cliff Sutter and I think Sidney Wood. He told my mother about that game lots of times, but it didn't mean much to her. She used to play tennis years ago, just for fun, but she wasn't too good and gave it up. Now the garden is the big thing with her, and she hardly ever comes out to their court, even to watch.

I play a game of tennis just like my father's. Oh, not as good. Not nearly as good, because I haven't had the experi-ence. I just haven't played as much. But it's the same game, really. I've had people tell me that when they saw us play-ing together — that we both made the same shot the same way. Maybe my backhand was a little better (when it was on), and I used to think that my old man didn't get down low enough on a soft return to his forehand. But mostly we played the same game. Which isn't surprising, seeing that he taught me the game. He started way back when I was about nine or ten. He used to spend whole mornings with me, teaching me a single shot. I guess it was good for me and he did teach me a good, all-around game, but even now I can remember that those morning lessons would somehow discourage both of us. I couldn't seem to learn fast enough to suit him, and he'd get upset and shout across at me "Straight arm! Straight arm!", and then *I'd* get jumpy and do the shot even worse. We'd both be glad when the lesson ended.

I don't mean to say that he was so *much* better than I was. We got so we played pretty close a lot of the time. I can still remember the day I first beat him at singles. It was in June of 1940. I'd been playing quite a lot at school and this was my first weekend home after school ended. We went out in the morning, no one else there, and, as usual, he walked right through me the first set — about 6-1 or so. I played much worse than my regular game then, just like I always did against him for some reason. But the next set I aced him in the second game and that set me up and I went on and took him, 7-5. It was a wonderful set of tennis and I was right on top of the world when it ended. I remember running all the way back to the house to tell Mother about it. The old man came in and sort of smiled at her and said something like "Well, I guess I'm old now, Amy."

But don't get the idea I started beating him then. That was the whole trouble. There I was, sixteen, seventeen years old and getting my size, and I began to think, Well, it's about time you took him. He was in his forties — not a young man any more. But he went right on beating me. Somehow I never played well against him and I knew it, and I'd start pressing and getting sore and of course my game would go blooey.

I remember one weekend when I was in college, before I went into the Army, a whole bunch of us drove down to Montclair in May for a weekend — my two roommates and three girls we knew. It was going to be a lot of fun. But then we went out for some tennis and of course my father was there. We all played some mixed doubles, just fooling around, and then he asked me if I wanted some singles. In that casual way of his. And of course it was 6-2, 6-3, or some such thing. The second set we were really hitting out against each other and the kids watching got real quiet, just as if it was Forest Hills. And then when we came off, Alice, my date, said something to me. About him, I mean. "I think your father is a remarkable man," she said. "Simply remarkable. Don't you think so?" Maybe she wanted to make me feel better about losing, but it was a dumb question. What could I say except yes?

It was while I was in college that I began to play golf a little. I liked the game and I even bought clubs and took a couple of lessons. I broke ninety one day and wrote home to my father about it. He'd never played golf and he wrote back with some little gag about its being an old man's game. Just kidding, you know, and I guess I should have expected it, but I was embarrassed to talk about golf at home after that. I wasn't really very good at it, anyway.

I played some squash in college, too, and even made the B team, but I didn't try out for the tennis team. That disappointed my father, I think, because I wasn't any good at football, and I think he wanted to see me make some team. So he could come and see me play and tell his friends about it, I guess. Still, we did play squash a few times and I could beat him, though I saw that with time he probably would have caught up with me.

I don't want you to get the idea from this that I didn't have a good time playing tennis with him. I can remember the good days very well — lots of days where we'd played some doubles with friends or even a set of singles where my game was holding up or maybe even where I'd taken one set. Afterward we'd walk back together through the orchard, with my father knocking the green apples off the path with his racket the way he always did and the two of us hot and sweaty while we smoked cigarettes and talked about lots of things. Then we'd sit on the veranda and drink a can of beer before taking a dip in the pool. We'd be very close then, I felt.

And I keep remembering a funny thing that happened years ago — oh, away back when I was thirteen or fourteen. We'd gone away, the three of us, for a month in New Hampshire in the summer. We played a lot of tennis that month and my game was coming along pretty fast, but of course my father would beat me every single time we played. Then he and I both entered the little town championship there the last week in August. Of course, I was put out in the first round (I was only a kid), but my old man went on into the finals. There was quite a big crowd that came to watch that day, and they had a referee and everything. My father was playing a young fellow — about twenty or twenty-one, I guess he was. I remember that I sat by myself, right down beside the court, to watch, and while they were warming up I looked at this man playing my father and whispered to myself, but almost out loud, "Take him! Take him!" I don't know why, but I just wanted him to beat my father in those finals, and it sort of

scared me when I found that out. I wanted him to give him
a real shellacking. Then they began to play and it was a
very close match for a few games. But this young fellow
was good, really good. He played a very controlled game,
waiting for errors and only hitting out for winners when
it was a sure thing. And he went on and won the first set,
and in the next my father began to hit into the net and it
was pretty plain that it wasn't even going to be close in
the second set. I kept watching and pretty soon I felt very
funny sitting there. Then the man won a love game off my
father and I began to shake. I jumped up and ran all the
way up the road to our cabin and into my room and lay
down on my bed and cried hard. I kept thinking how I'd
wanted to have the man win, and I knew it was about
the first time I'd ever seen my father lose a love game. I
never felt so ashamed. Of course, that was years and years
ago.

I don't think any of this would have bothered me except
for one thing — I've always *liked* my father. Except for
this game, we've always gotten along fine. He's never
wanted a junior-partner son. He's never been one for pro-
nouncements or easy advice, and he's no backslapper, thank
God. We've argued about hundreds of things, I guess, but
they're the kind of arguments you enjoy because you know
the other man is interested, paying attention. There have
been times where I didn't see much of him for a year or
so, but when we got together (at a ball game, say, or during
a long trip in a car), we've always found we could talk and
argue and have a lot of laughs, too. In 1944, when I came
back on my last furlough before I went overseas, I found

that he'd chartered a sloop. The two of us went off for a week's cruise along the Maine coast, and it was fine. Early-morning swims and trying to cook over charcoal and the wonderful quiet that comes over those little coves after you've anchored for the night and the wind has dropped and perhaps you're getting ready to shake up some cocktails. One night there, when we were sitting on deck and smoking cigarettes in the dark, he told me something that he never even told my mother — that he'd tried to get into the Army and had been turned down. He just said it and we let it drop, but I've always been glad he told me. Somehow it made me feel better about going overseas.

Naturally, during the war I didn't play any tennis at all. And when I came back I got married and all, and I was older, so of course the game didn't mean as much to me. But still, the first weekend we played at my father's — the very first time I'd played him in four years — it was the same as ever. And I'd have sworn I had outgrown the damn thing. But Janet, my wife, had never seen me play the old man before and *she* spotted something. She came up to our room when I was changing afterward. "What's the matter with you?" she asked me. "Why does it mean so much to you? It's just a game, isn't it? I can see it's a big thing for your father. That's why he plays so much and that's why he's so good at it. But why you?" She was half kidding, but I could see that it upset her. "This isn't a contest," she said. "We're not voting for Best Athlete in the County, are we?" I took her up on that and tried to explain the thing a little, but she wouldn't try to understand. "I just don't like a sorehead," she told me as she went out of the room.

I guess that brings me down to last summer and what happened. I had been away in Oregon for five and a half years, where I was the West Coast divisional manager for my company, and except for a few quick visits East, I hadn't seen much of my parents. Then, near the end of summer, I was transferred back to the main office, and we came back and found a house out on Long Island. My mother invited us out for a family weekend, but Janet and I were still settling in, so we just came on Sunday. It was late in September, one of those wonderful days where it begins to get a little cool and the air is so bright. It was funny going back to the old place. The house had gotten smaller and, in a way, so had my mother and father. I had the odd feeling that I had become a stranger — a grown man visiting just anybody's house.

Father had played his usual four or five sets of doubles Saturday, and the next day he had his regular tennis gang there — Eddie Earnshaw and Mark O'Connor and that Mr. Lacy. I guess we men had played three sets of doubles, changing around, and we were sitting there catching our breath. I was waiting for Father to ask me for our singles. But he'd told me earlier that he hadn't been able to get much sleep the night before, so I'd decided that he was too tired for singles. Of course, I didn't even mention that out loud in front of the others — it would have embarrassed him. Then I looked around and noticed that my father was sitting in one of those canvas chairs instead of standing up, the way he usually did between sets. He looked awfully pale, even under his tan, and while I was looking at him he suddenly leaned over and grabbed his stomach and was sick on the grass. We all knew it was pretty bad, and we laid him down and put his cap over his eyes, and I ran back to the house to tell Mother and phone up the doctor. Father didn't say a word when we carried him into the house in the chair, and then Dr. Stockton came and said it was a heart attack and that Father had played his last game of tennis.

You would have thought after that and after all those months in bed that my father would just give up his tennis court — have it plowed over or let it go to grass. But Janet and I went out there for the weekend just last month and I was surprised to find that the court was in good shape, and Father said that he had asked the gang to come over, just so I could have some good men's doubles. He'd even had a chair set up in the orchard, halfway out to the court, so he could walk out there by himself. He walked out slow, the way he has to, and then sat down in the chair and rested for a couple of minutes, and then made it the rest of the way.

I haven't been playing much tennis this year, but I was really on my game there that day at my father's. I don't think I've ever played better on that court. I hardly made an error and I was relaxed and I felt good about my game. The others even spoke about how well I played.

But somehow it wasn't much fun. It just didn't seem like a real contest to me, and I didn't really care that I was holding my serve right along and winning my sets no matter who my partner was. Maybe for the first time in my life, I guess, I found out that it was only a game we were playing — only that and no more. And I began to realize what

my old man and I had done to that game. I'd never wanted
to beat him — not really. I think I had only wanted him to
notice me, but he'd been too busy living up to something
he'd promised himself a long time before. All that time, all
those years, I had only been trying to grow up and he had
been trying to keep young, and we'd both done it on the
tennis court. And now our struggle was over. I found that
out that day, and when I did I suddenly wanted to tell my
father about it. But then I looked over at him, sitting in a
chair with a straw hat on his head, and I decided not to. I
noticed that he didn't seem to be watching us at all. I had
the feeling, instead, that he was *listening* to us play tennis
and perhaps imagining a game to himself or remembering
how he would play the point — the big, high-bouncing
serve and the rush to the net for the volley, and then going
back for the lob and looking up at it and the wonderful
feeling as you uncoil on the smash and put the ball away.

Children at the Shore

"DOES anybody mind fish chowder?" Lucille Balchen asked as she came out onto the porch carrying an Old-Fashioned in one hand and pulling a wisp of hair out of her eyes with the other. "It's sort of a Maine specialty and I thought . . . Anyway, that's what we're having." Automatically, she bent down to pick up a pair of wet, sandy sneakers that were lying in front of the screen door, balanced them toe to toe in the sun on the porch railing, and then sat down on the steps beside her brother-in-law, Peter Mottram. "My God, but I hate a kitchen on a day like this," she sighed.

"Yes, *I* mind fish chowder," said Barnaby, who was seven and who was sprawled on his back on an old Army cot with his bare feet in the air. "I mind it very much. It's disgusting."

"I didn't mean you," his mother said. "I meant your aunt and uncle. You'll eat five bowls if you get the chance, so I'm not too worried about you."

"Yes, just shut up, Barney," said his sister Christine. "Look at your feet! Talk about disgusting." She was tall for fifteen — already taller than her mother — very tan in her shorts, and her blond hair was short and tousled. She was passing a plate of crackers, and when she got to Lucille she bent down and asked, "Could I have an Old-Fashioned, Mother?"

"By no means," Lucille said calmly. "What a question. There's Coke on the back porch, I think."

"Oh, Mother! *That's* not what I meant. Just this once." She turned to Mottram. "I'll bet all the girls at Northeast Harbor have a drink once in a while, don't they, Uncle Pete? Just in the *family*, at least?"

"Well, not when we were there," Mottram said, laughing. "At least, I didn't see them. There wasn't anybody quite your age where we were visiting, but I did hear some gossip about all the fifteen-year-olds giving up Old-Fashioneds. Martinis are the thing this summer."

Tinka, the other Balchen child, who was eleven, guffawed loudly, and Christine walked silently across the porch and gave a cracker from the plate to the Scottie who lay in the corner. "Here, John," she said softly. "Old John." For a moment, Mottram wondered whether he had hurt Christine's feelings, and then he gave up the problem. He wasn't accustomed to large, cluttered families, or, for that matter, to talking to children. And he did not, after all, know the Balchens very well. Lucille Balchen was his wife's sister, and she was six years older than Marie. In the winters, the Balchens lived just outside Chicago, where Ted Balchen had a job with a small company that published college textbooks; in the summers, they came to this cottage at Green Cove, on the Maine coast. The Mottrams, who were childless and had spent the previous two summers in Europe and the one before that in East Hampton, were making their first visit.

They had arrived by car the night before from Northeast Harbor, where they had stayed a week with a college classmate of Mottram's, a man who had bought a forty-five-foot power cruiser that spring as a surprise birthday present for his wife. When Marie received a letter from Lucille asking them to Green Cove but explaining that, because of the size of the cottage, they would have to stay at a small hotel three miles away, she and Mottram had agreed to spend just two days with the Balchens. "I have no idea what it'll be like," Marie had said. "But after all she *is* my sister and you know how long it's been."

Now, sipping his drink and looking at Lucille, Mottram wondered about the two sisters. Lucille was wearing blue jeans that were too small for her and a faded pink blouse with a ruffled collar. She was shorter than Marie and distinctly plump, and Mottram was perfectly sure that his wife would not have streaked, graying hair when she reached Lucille's age. What a few years, he thought, to make such a difference. How many defeats and small discouragements, he speculated, does it take to make a woman lose her looks? How many days of tiredness, of doctors called in the night, of debts added up and bills postponed? How many meals prepared and cleared away, how many knees bandaged, tempers calmed, requests considered and denied, and how many snowsuits let out before a woman begins to forget about her hair and to let her nails go and to converse with her guests with her eyes always turning toward her children in that harassed, affectionate look that seems at once to count them and to touch them lightly? Mottram did not have to look across the porch to where his wife was talking with Ted Balchen to make the comparison. In the four years they had been married — years in which Mottram's annual salary as an advertising executive in television had gone from fifteen to forty-three thousand dollars — Marie's appearance had been changed only by the clothes she had worn. She had taken to those new, clever, and expensive clothes just as she had taken to the new seven-room apartment on Sixty-first Street and to the two servants and to the Lincoln convertible and to the lunches at "21" and Pavillon and to the small dinners for twelve and the large cocktail parties for fifty and (he suspected) to the whispered, hand-holding meetings for two in obscure, late restaurants and dark bars — with no apparent awkwardness or excitement, with no sign that this was anything more than she had expected. In those four years, Mottram had seen his wife's face in moments of interest, passion, boredom, anger, drunkenness, sleep, laughter, avarice, and scorn, and he knew that it was a face not likely ever to change from its customary flat and startling beauty.

Mottram shook his head slightly. He had slept badly the night before in the strange hotel bed, and he realized that he hadn't been listening to Lucille. "It can't be called a resort," she was saying, "and thank goodness for that. Just a dozen summer cottages or so, and the general store and the float. There are only about ten boats in the harbor, not counting the lobstermen. The best thing, of course, is that there are lots of kids here, and that makes it perfect for ours. They're off visiting most of the day." She finished her drink, looked at her watch, and gave her children the same quick, encompassing glance that Mottram had noticed before. "Has anybody seen Jasper?" she asked vaguely.

"He was down at the beach a little while ago," Tinka said from deep in a comic book. "He'd dug something up and rolled in it. He smelled awful."

"Jasper?" Mottram repeated. "Don't tell me you have another dog!"

"Oh, yes. A beagle. He's Tinka's life," Lucille explained. "John belongs to Chris; they're just the same age, which makes him awfully old. The cat is Barney's, but she spends all her time sleeping on our bed." She gave a despairing little laugh. "We had a parakeet last winter, but it died, thank God."

"Jasper went to the vet," Tinka said proudly. "He pulled out a *hundred and four quills*. I have some upstairs. I'll get them and show you." She jumped up and ran into the house, letting the screen door bang behind her.

"While you're there, get your sweater and bathing suit," Lucille called after her. "You're due at the Sandersons' for the picnic in ten minutes. And go to the bathroom."

"Died of a heart attack. Died of a heart attack. Died of a heart attack," Barnaby intoned from the cot.

"*What?*" said Mottram.

"Johnny Sanderson's grandmother died of a heart attack," he announced. "Last winter. Boom! Curtains."

"That'll be quite enough of that," Lucille said as she stood up. "Where are your glasses, Barney?"

"I don't know. Lost again. Upstairs somewhere, I guess."

"Well, get them and put them on. Lunch in five minutes, everybody." She paused for a moment, looking out at the shining water of the bay, and then sighed and picked up

Tinka's comic book from the floor and went into the house. Mottram, who was beginning to feel sleepy from the whiskey and the cool, wind-blown air, got up and stretched, and then joined Ted and Christine and his wife at the end of the porch.

"Little Bear, Great Bear, Egg Rock, Gull, Gray Head, and Martin's," Ted was saying as he pointed to the row of low, tree-covered islands that stretched down the long bay. "That last one is the point, and way out, on a clear day, you can see Shag Rock Light. You can sail for days here and never see open water."

"It's lovely, simply lovely," said Marie, looking at her long and perfect legs crossed before her on the deck chair.

"Can you see your boat from here?" Mottram asked.

"Sure." Ted pointed down to the cove almost directly below the house, where a half dozen small sailboats pitched at their moorings, their bare masts swinging and circling against the bright water. "It's the second one there. She's just a cat we chartered, but Chris is learning to sail."

"Learning! Learning!" Christine echoed. "It's my second whole summer. And I'll take you on any time. Any old time you want to race, Pop. You can borrow another boat and I'll give *you* a lesson."

"I didn't know you chartered a catboat," Mottram said. "I thought just yachts."

"No, the size doesn't matter," Ted said. "You can charter a rowboat, for that matter. We'll take you out for a sail tomorrow if it doesn't blow too hard. Right now, it's freshening up pretty fast from the southwest, and that's apt to last two or three days." He stood up and flicked his cigarette over the porch railing. "We better go in and eat now if you and I are going to play golf, Pete. I think you should reconsider, though. It's been three or four years for me and you know I haven't even got any clubs."

"Not at all, Ted. You'll probably murder me," Mottram said uncomfortably. "What are you going to do this afternoon, Chris?"

"I don't know. Pop won't let me caddie for you. Mope around, I guess. Play softball. Play Hearts again with Barney and watch him cheat." She put her arm through her father's and leaned her soft head on his shoulder as they followed Marie through the screen door.

After lunch, the family scattered with what, to Mottram, seemed remarkable haste. Tinka had gone to her picnic, and Barnaby, not wanting to finish his dessert, found a fishing line on his father's desk and departed for the float, announcing that he was going to catch enough flounders for the family's breakfast. Lucille and Marie went off in the Mottrams' car to the hairdresser's, ten miles away, where Marie was going to treat her sister to a permanent. Mottram and Ted Balchen drove off in the opposite direction to the golf course, leaving Christine, who had announced that she might give the Scottie a bath.

"I don't see how you keep track of them all," Mottram said to his brother-in-law, a little confused by all the scattered objectives and directions of the afternoon.

"Neither do I," Ted said, smiling. "Somehow they all show up for supper, though. Everybody keeps busy."

The golf was a failure. Ted Balchen, sharing Mottram's

clubs, shot an eight and a nine on the first two holes, losing three balls in the process. By the time they had played nine holes, the caddie was obviously disgusted. The wind, which had been increasing in force all afternoon and toward the end was even affecting Mottram's effortless, efficient game, gave them the excuse to quit.

Driving back in the Balchens' old station wagon, Ted was apologetic. "I guess that's the end of *my* golf career," he said. "I never was a threat to Snead anyway."

"Nonsense," Mottram said curtly. "You hadn't played, and they were strange clubs, and this is a hell of a wind."

"No, the clubs were wonderful. They're just about the finest set I ever saw, let alone played with. Anyway, the game is really too expensive for me, so it's just as well." He laughed briefly. "A caddie's scorn is a terrible thing."

"Oh, hell. That little twirp."

Balchen, who was driving a little too fast on the narrow road, began to talk quickly. "Listen, Pete," he said. "While we're on the subject of expenses, I want to tell you how I feel about that loan. I really hated to do it, but I couldn't see any other way just then, what with Barney's tonsils and Lucille down with the flu and all. It came all at once there, and I guess you know we publishing people don't get much opportunity to build up a contingency fund. In any case, you saved our lives with the five hundred, and I'm going to get it back to you before this year is over."

"Don't give it a thought," Mottram said, looking away from Ted. He had been hoping Balchen wouldn't bring this subject up. "You know I wanted to do it, and my job is — well, it's a fantastic business. We're all overpaid."

"No, I really mean it," Ted said doggedly. "Right now, you see, I'm trying to do something about Christine's education. You know, she's finished first-year high, but our local high school out there is just not good. I don't know why, except our town isn't a big, rich place like Winnetka or Evanston. But there's a day school in the next town, a private place that's first-rate, and Lucille and I are trying to swing that. You see, Chris has got a really good mind, although it's a little scattered right now, and this is one thing we *have* to do somehow. If I can just get this book of mine polished off this month. It won't sell much, of course — too pedantic — but it'll help. It's pretty hard to get much work done here, though, what with the kids around. Tinka's trying to learn to type. On my machine. I go back to the office in two weeks. And I have to help Lucille while I'm here, and the rowboat needs painting."

"Sure," Mottram said. "Sure." Why don't you just shut up, he thought. Just keep quiet about it all. He wasn't used to hearing apologies and nervous confessions. It was not done among his business friends, who talked always, at lunches and in taxis and in offices, with loud confidence and optimism. Optimism was part of the trade. Mottram knew he was feeling childishly·upset over the ruined golf game, and he was angry at himself because he felt he had shown his disappointment and had been rude to Ted. The trouble with me, he thought, lighting a cigarette and looking out the window, is just being here with this damned big family, with all its complications and its hundreds of daily plans and its unpainted rowboats and its self-love and self-sufficiency and its sloppiness and its no money. I don't care about the loan. I don't give a damn about it, except that's all they need me for. I don't know what I'm doing here. He thought back to the night before, when he and Marie had lain on their uncomfortable hotel beds, smoking in the dark in the stuffy room while Marie talked about her sister. "It's just *pathetic*," she had said. "And grim, besides. Why, Lucille used to be so lovely, and she took such pains with herself. She was in dramatics at Smith, you know. And she was so — I don't know — exciting. I used to copy her in everything she did. And now look at her — why, I don't even think she reads the newspaper any more. Of course, the children are sweet. But it's sad, actually, sad. I'm going to send her a new dress for her birthday, an expensive one. I don't care what she says."

And Mottram remembered another remark of his wife's, something she had said at a dinner party in New York a month or two before. "The ultimate hayseed rudeness," she had said, smiling faintly and holding her cigarette beside her face as she always did when she had an audience, "is the infliction of family love on one's guest. All those homely, awful intimacies. Smiling at Baby LeRoy while he passes the Planters Peanuts at cocktails and spills them on your dress. Kleenex on the coffee table. The poodle who just *will not* learn not to jump up on the guests. Instant coffee and the passing cheerful remark about the unpaid dentist's bill. Sonny permitted just a sip of the ninety-eight-cent wine while we eat the spaghetti dinner. Dad putting sister Anne to bed while Mother darns socks and smiles at the beauty of it all. Lord!" There had been laughter.

They turned off the road onto the sandy driveway and

drove between pine trees up to the cottage. "I'll get us a beer," Balchen said, going into the kitchen. "Everybody seems to be away." Mottram took his golf clubs out of the car and carefully stood them beside the back door, next to an old pair of oars. When, a little later, the two men stepped out on the front porch, the wind, sweeping off the torn, sun-flecked bay and up to the house, struck Mottram with sudden force and banged the screen door shut behind him. All the windows were rattling, and Mottram shivered with sudden cold when he looked down at the cove and saw the little boats bucking and rocking violently as they tore at the moorings and dipped their stubby bows under the white water. Standing beside him, Balchen suddenly put his beer can down. "Oh, hell!" he exclaimed. "Boat's gone. Probably dragged her mooring right down to the end of the harbor. I hope she hasn't fetched up on the rocks. Come on. We'll go down to the float, where we can see her, and then row down and try to make her fast to something. Probably the kids are down there now."

But the float was empty when they got there. They stood on its wet, moving surface while Balchen peered down the cove and the gangplank roller squeaked and banged behind them with every motion of the waves. "That's funny," Ted said at last. "I can't see her." He was frowning as he turned to Mottram, the wind ruffling his short gray hair. "Listen," he said, "I'm going up and find the kids. Maybe they know what's happened. You stay here and keep looking. She'll be hard to see because we're so close to the water. You don't suppose . . ." He turned and ran up the gangplank.

Mottram stood there for ten minutes, bracing himself against the uneasy motion, and shading his eyes as he stared downwind at the empty, rock-strewn shore at the end of the little harbor. When Ted reappeared, he had a pair of binoculars around his neck, and there were two men with him, one of whom looked as if he had just arisen from a nap. They hurried down the gangplank. Ted introduced them quickly, but Mottram failed to catch the names in the wind. Ted's face looked white and pinched. "We can't seem to find anything out," he said. "Nobody saw them go, but it looks now as if Chris and the two Quigg boys went out in the boat. But nobody saw them." His voice was flat and preoccupied, and his eyes kept sweeping along the edge of the cove as he talked. "Tinka's still off on her picnic somewhere. Barney says he heard them talking about going for a sail, but he didn't pay much attention. Lucille's not back yet, but Homer Quigg is telephoning the Coast Guard, just in case. If you come with me, we'll hop in the car and drive down toward the point and see if we can see them. I'll need you to look while I drive." He turned to the other men, whose khaki pants and blue jeans were already wet from the waves that were splashing up over the windward side of the float. "One of you might walk around to the lee shore there and look. Jim, why don't you drive into the village and try to rout out Bascom and Gray and McHugh and the other lobstermen and see if they'll put out and look? Tell them I'll pay, of course. I think they're all back from their runs by now."

"They won't take pay," the man said as he started up the gangplank. He turned back to Balchen for a moment.

"Don't let it get you, Ted," he said. "They're probably somewhere else altogether. Well find them quick."

Mottram felt helpless and frightened as he hurried up the hill toward the house behind Ted. "Is it very dangerous?" he asked stupidly while they were climbing into the car.

Balchen slammed the station wagon back in a tight curve and scraped the gears as he swung down the driveway. "It's *God-damned* dangerous," he said shortly. "Those kids have no business at all out there today, and when I find them I'm going to fix them for fair. None of them can sail well enough for this kind of weather, and they know it. We've got rules about this. I just hope we spot them before Lucille gets back. I'll put Chris on shore for the rest of the summer. Just wait and see if I don't!"

For the next three quarters of an hour, Balchen drove at tremendous speed down the narrow macadam road that paralleled the bay, stopping whenever they came to the top of an open hill and turning often onto dirt roads that led out to wooded points. Here he would leap out and seize the binoculars from Mottram. "They'd be down here," he would mutter as he swung the glasses back and forth. "They couldn't get anywhere beating upwind on a day like this." Once, as they were driving along, he banged the steering wheel with his fist and cried, "God-damned kids!" On the straight stretches of the road, he kept saying to Mottram, "Look behind the islands. Look back at each island. They might be outside there or beached." Once they did see a scrap of white just nosing out from behind a rocky point, and Balchen slammed on the brakes. But there were two sails, not one; it was a yawl, tacking up the bay with her mainsail dropped and making slow progress against the wind. When they reached the gravelly beach at the end of the last point, Balchen spent five minutes staring at the sea of empty, uneasy water that stretched to the east of them. Finally, he lowered the binoculars and turned back to the car. "They wouldn't have come this far," he said quietly. "Not in the whole afternoon." Just as he started to climb into the car, he began to tremble jerkily and dropped the glasses on the road. There was a tinkle of glass, and Balchen slowly bent and picked up the ruined binoculars. "I'm sorry," he said, and when he turned, Mottram could see that he had tears in his eyes. "You drive back, will you, Pete?"

"Sure," Mottram said, glad of something to do. "Sure thing." Going back, he drove as fast as he dared, but the sun was low now and directly in his eyes, and the wind kept buffeting and tearing at the car. "Don't give up, Ted," he said again and again. "Probably they'll be there. Probably they'll be home when we get back. That's often the way, isn't it?" Balchen said nothing, and Mottram could feel the rapid pulsing of his own heart and the sweat of his hands on the steering wheel.

But it was clear when the two men got to the float that they hadn't turned up. There must have been a dozen people around the gangplank, and there were so many men and women and children standing on the float that the waves were washing right across its outer edge. Two dachshunds were running back and forth in the crowd, yapping wildly. The younger children, in red or yellow life jackets, had bright, excited eyes. Mottram looked for Lucille in the crowd and saw her at last at one corner of the float. She was smiling determinedly, with her arms folded tightly across her waist, and her new permanent was all wrong. "They're getting a plane," a woman said in a high voice to Balchen as he came down the gangplank. Everyone turned to look at him. "The Coast Guard is sending a plane and all the boats are out." Balchen did not go at once to his wife. He spoke quietly to a man in steel-rimmed glasses who was sucking an unlit pipe. They both looked out toward the bay for a moment, and then Balchen went over to Lucille. They smiled vaguely and awkwardly at each other, and Balchen reached out and steadied her against the motion of the float. "Tinka is still at the Sandersons'," Lucille said, as if she were reporting an ordinary afternoon's event. "She doesn't know yet. Barney's having supper at the McKinnons'. The Quiggs are staying by the telephone. Everyone — everyone's been so nice."

"You better go home and make some coffee," Balchen said. "It's getting cold here." And then, as the two of them started for the gangplank, with all the others stepping back quickly to make room for them, Balchen said, "Your hair looks very nice."

Mottram glanced around for his wife and saw her standing on the dock above the gangplank, looking frightened and beautiful and out of place in her elegant, trim slacks and sandals. A moment later, a high-bowed lobster boat appeared at the head of the cove, bore swiftly down on them, and made a circle back up to the float. "I need a man," the fisherman shouted as he throttled his engine down and came alongside, the boat pitching and slapping in the waves. "I've been two miles up and now I'm headin' down behind the Bears. It'll be dark in an hour and I need a man to look with me." There was an uncertain pause among all the people on the float, and Mottram, who didn't want to talk to his wife just then, said "I'll go," and quickly ran and jumped the narrow space between the boat and the float and landed on his knees on the wet, slippery deck.

The moment they cleared the mouth of the cove, Mottram felt the full, shuddering force of the wind. It caught suddenly at the bow of the boat and swung it off course. They heeled heavily and then, as the fisherman spun the wheel over, a wave broke against the hull and showered Mottram's head and shoulders. He shivered at the impact of the icy water. "Better get below and put on that old jacket I got there!" the man shouted to him. "Then you can stand up beside me behind the windshield here. Keep drier that way." It was almost dark in the tiny cabin, but Mottram could see a scrap of old flowered carpeting under his feet as he struggled with the stiff denim jacket. The place smelled powerfully of fish and gasoline. Mottram stood there for a minute before he went back up to the wind. Bracing himself against the motion of the boat, his head touching the low deckhouse ceiling, he suddenly felt, under the throbbing of the engine and the cruel jarring of the waves, the great, uneasy power of the force beneath him, the blind shouldering of the dark and depthless sea itself that now moved him and held him trapped and somehow sustained him upon its frail and treacherous surface. For the first time, he thought of Chris and not her parents, and the idea of her wandering somewhere about this cold deep, and now probably forever lost and alone, sent a great surge of terror and excitement and loneliness through him. Abruptly he bolted back up the steps to the light and the wind.

They stayed out for almost two hours. Twice they were sure they saw a beached sailboat on the next island and were wrong. And then, just before dark, they spotted what appeared to be a mast on an even more distant shore. The two of them stared at it and said nothing as they came closer and closer in the gathering darkness, although both had known for some minutes now that it was only a bare, dead pine above the rocks. At last, the boat owner, whose name was Bascom, put the wheel over and they headed back for the cove. The wind had dropped somewhat with the coming of night, and it was almost quiet now except for the pulsing of the engine in the darkness. Once Mottram asked, "If they had capsized, would you find them now? I mean — if they were in the water?"

"No, the bodies wouldn't float yet," Bascom said. "Probably fetch up on the lee shore somewhere in a couple of days. That sailboat would keep afloat for a while, though. Has a little airtight compartment forward. Don't know if they had life belts." He spat carefully over the side and then bent forward to make some adjustment to the engine.

Mottram leaned his head and arms against the cold, throbbing surface of the deckhouse and felt a burst of exhaustion and disgusted, unreasoning anger. "God damn them!" he whispered to himself. Damn them all — the whole family — with their love and their defenselessness and their sloppiness. They're always losing things — dogs, eyeglasses, belongings — and now they've lost a child. They're careless people. They leave their clothes around, their dinner plates are cracked, and their car isn't washed. They're careless about money and about lives. Where do they get their stupid faith, their notion that everything is going to turn out all right and that somebody will look after them? People like that should be frightened all the time. They have nothing, nothing that's safe at all. And for the first time it occurred to him that he would have to stay longer than two days now, and that he would probably have to pay for the funeral. He wished he were back home, back in his office.

"Coming in now," Bascom said quietly. Mottram looked up and saw the lights of the houses along the shore. Bascom throttled down the engine as they came into the cove. Then he leaned forward sharply and peered off into the darkness. "Hand me that flashlight there," he said to Mottram. "Just inside there, to your left." Mottram found the light and gave it to Bascom, and the beam suddenly leaped out, searched along the oily-looking waves, and came to rest on the white hull of a sailboat, moving gently up and down at her mooring. "There she is," Bascom said gently. "Safe and sound."

"What?" Mottram said. "What is it?"

"That's her," Bascom said. He turned and clapped Mottram on the back. "Looks like we missed our suppers for nothing! I guess Marv Gray or one of the others towed them back while we were outside. I'll just drop you off at the float now. Tell Mrs. Balchen I'm sure pleased. We never had a drowning here, you know. Not in summer."

Shivering with cold, Mottram stumbled up the dark path toward the cottage. He passed a lighted house and heard a child calling to its mother from the top floor. He stopped and looked at his watch and found that it was almost nine-thirty, and then tripped over a rock and cursed. All his anger now was turned toward Christine. "I'll bet they fix *her* wagon!" he muttered to himself. "I hope he takes a strap to her, the little fool."

When he opened the kitchen door, he thought for a moment he had come to the wrong house. A radio was playing music loudly somewhere in the front of the house, and the living room was full of laughter and loud words. Then the two dogs (the beagle had turned up) came barking and jumping out to him, and then they were all around him — Chris, Lucille, Ted, Tinka, Barnaby, all smiling and laughing and explaining. He blinked his eyes in the light, feeling like a stupid party guest who has failed to guess a charade and has had to have it explained to him by the winning team.

"She wasn't lost at all!" Barnaby shouted above the others. "They went ashore!"

"She beached on Grassy Neck," Lucille said. For some reason, she had a large bandage on her forehead. "You couldn't see them from the road."

"They were being towed back when you went out with Bascom."

"They were being blown down and knew they couldn't get back, so they just went ashore."

"Marv Gray found them. They've been back for *hours*. The Quiggs just left — didn't you see them?"

"I was on the radio, Uncle Pete! They were talking about us on the radio!" It was Christine. Her hair was still damp, her cheeks were bright red, and her eyes were huge with excitement. "Isn't that a *scream?* They thought we were lost."

"Very funny," Mottram said. "I hope you know how your parents felt. And me. Anyway, I'm glad you're back." As they went into the living room, Ted took his arm and said, "Thanks, Pete. You know how we feel. And don't worry about Chris. She's still a little keyed up right now. Her mother and I are going over this whole damned thing with her tomorrow. We'll straighten her out." But Mottram noticed that even Ted had a permanent, fatuous smile on his face.

Marie was sitting in a wicker chair by the fire with a drink in her hand. "Hi," she said. "We were about to send the Coast Guard after *you*. What was all that sudden leaping into boats, anyway? We could have used you more around here." She looked pale and annoyed.

Mottram began to shiver again, and Ted poured him a drink and then took him upstairs and gave him a dry flannel shirt. Mottram towelled his back vigorously in the bathroom, but there was still a cold, shocked expression in his eyes when he looked in the mirror. He finished his drink and went downstairs. Somebody had turned off the radio, and Marie was alone in the living room. Looking for another drink, he went to the kitchen. As he pushed the door open, he saw Lucille and Chris bending over a cookbook together. They were giggling about something and when they saw him in the doorway they both stopped suddenly, like children caught at some game. Even with Lucille's bandage and tight permanent, the mother and daughter looked extraordinarily alike. They both looked very young. "Hi!" Lucille said. "We're having steak! We borrowed some from the Sandersons' freeze. We decided everybody needed a big meal tonight. How are you on making hollandaise?"

Dinner was noisy with accounts and recapitulations of the afternoon. The dogs were given the steak bones from the table. During dessert, Tinka bent lower and lower over her strawberries and then unexpectedly burst into loud wails. "Nobody *told* me!" she cried. "There I was at the picnic and nobody came and *told* me! My own sister might have been dead and I would have been eating clams without ever *knowing!*" For some reason, this set all the Balchens off into bursts of laughter, and Mottram found himself laughing in nervous shouts. A moment later, Ted took Barnaby upstairs to bed. "I didn't get any flounders," Mottram heard him complain to his father. "Not a single bite."

"The tide was wrong, Barney," Ted said gently. "We'll go in the morning and get some, you and I. But you'll have to wear your glasses tomorrow, see?"

The Mottrams didn't talk driving back to their hotel. Mottram felt exhausted and empty, and one of his eyelids wouldn't stop twitching. The moment they got to their hotel room, Marie slammed the door behind her. "I need a drink," she said in an angry voice, "and so do you." She came back from the bathroom with two glasses half filled with water, opened Mottram's suitcase, and took out the bottle of Scotch. Mottram put his golf clubs in a corner and stretched out in a chair, his legs in front of him and a hand over his eyes. He had never felt so tired — not even in the Army. "Here," Marie said, handing him his drink. She lit a cigarette, shook out the match, and sat down facing him on one of the beds, with her legs drawn up and an ashtray beside her.

"Have you *ever* in all your *life?*" she began. "I was appalled, *appalled!* A party! They had a party! Why they're — they're nothing but babies, the whole bunch of them. That Christine still doesn't know what she did. She probably never will, if I'm any judge. Do you know, Pete, how Lucille got that cut over her eye?"

"No," Mottram said. He was having a hard time concentrating on what his wife was saying. "How?"

"She passed out, that's how. Right in the living room. It was just after you left in the boat. She simply broke down and wept and said that she was a bad mother and that she couldn't stand it, and then she passed out. She hit her head on the floor or something and got a tremendous lump and there was blood all over the place. It absolutely terrified me. And then when she came to, she began apologizing to everybody. Isn't that just awful? I cried myself then." She flicked a cigarette ash into the tray and took a long drink.

Even sitting on a hotel bed she looks poised, Mottram thought vaguely. She turns her head just right, even talking about this.

"But I shall *never* recover from this evening," Marie went on. "Steak! As if they could afford steak! Why, Lucille told me at the hairdresser's about their money thing.

I simply do not understand them. Thank God we're leaving soon. This family —"

"Oh, shut up!" Mottram shouted suddenly. He put his drink on the floor and stood up. "What do you know about it, anyway? What do either of us know about it? How do we know what *we'd* do? You with your answers and your damned parlor analysis!" He walked across the room, opened a door, and stepped out onto the little porch outside their room, shutting the door behind him.

It was cold on the porch and there was still a breath of wind somewhere in the darkness above him. Mottram put his hands in his pockets as he stared out at the shadowy trees. For a moment, he felt nothing at all except the cold and his exhaustion. And then, for some reason, he remembered the sharp, quick look Lucille and Chris had given him that evening when he had come upon them laughing together in the kitchen — a sudden twin expression of secretiveness and hostility, the insiders' look. And he remembered the thought he had had a moment ago — the odd, frightening idea that had made him shout at his wife. Sitting in there, listening to her cold voice in that ugly, too neat room, his eye had fallen on his hand-stitched leather golf bag, with its shining, grass-smudged irons and its matched woods, and he had been struck violently by the thought that this was the most he had to lose in the world, that this very golf set was the most valuable possession he owned. How ridiculous, he told himself now. It was a childish, exhausted night thought, born of his remembered fear and his fatigue. He had plenty of belongings, plenty of connections. But his mind would not let it alone. It ran on, a frantic, sweating searcher, opening bureau drawers in his New York apartment, riffling his thick checkbooks, banging the doors to the closets where his neat, expensive suits were hung, then brushing past his wife to run downstairs to look in the car, to fly through the papers on his office desk while it hunted, hunted for something — one object or harmony or attachment worth more to him than his silly golf clubs. He knew it now: he had too few possessions, he was traveling too light. Standing on the porch in the dark, Mottram put his hands to his face and tasted, on the inside of his wrist, the dead, acrid flavor of dried salt water.

Just a Matter of Time

NOBODY likes adventures. Oh, we think we do, but we're just fooling ourselves — telling ourselves that we're still young and curious and eager for surprises. The truth is that we're so deathly scared of anything strange that we don't even like to hear about it. I know, because nobody will listen to me. I'm fifty-two years old, steady in my ways and not a liar, and last fall, after I was knocked down by something that was more than unusual — by something that was plain impossible — I tried to tell people about it. Since then, I've decided that crazy things like this may happen all the time and that the only reason you don't hear about them is because the person involved learns to keep quiet. Three or four times, I've started to tell somebody about this, at lunch or after dinner in one of my clubs, but once I get into the middle of it the man I'm talking to begins to look at me in the damnedest way, as if he were embarrassed or something, and then I have to stop and say, "Look, there's nothing wrong with *me*. All this happened, just the way I'm telling you." So you stop talking about it. But it sticks there, inside, and you can't get rid of it. At first, you think that there must be some sensible explanation for the whole thing. Maybe Cromartie simply wrote down the wrong address that night. Or maybe it was his idea of a joke. But then, later on, you begin to wonder if there has to be a logical answer like that. Why not accept the simplest explanation of all? That's the way I look at it now.

Anybody who wants to check up on my story can ask Carol Cain. She was in on the beginning of it. And then there's my sister, down in Pennsylvania. You could ask her, though probably she thought I was only liquored-up the night I tried to take her to a place that didn't exist. But I don't care; these are the facts, and you'll just have to accept them until I find Cromartie. And I *will* find him some day. I'm sure of that.

First of all, you have to know about me and Carol Cain. I guess, looking at it honestly, I have to admit that that's probably all over for good. But back last fall, Carol and I seemed pretty well set. It looked like a steady thing. There are lots of girls like Carol in this town, and in a funny way I think I love them all — the pretty, lonely, bright, hardworking girls getting along in their thirties, who have made a kind of life for themselves in the city. You can see them on Park and Madison just after nine in the mornings, on their way to work, dressed in their imitation Balenciagas and carrying their folded *Times*, and looking brave and lovely as they wait for the light to change. Like most of those girls, Carol wants something solid now. You know — something better than this month's young man, whether he's the kind who wants to drag her down to one of those dirty Beat cellars in the Village, or the one who just likes to stay in and drink up all her Scotch, or the one who keeps her up until three in the morning while he talks about his analyst and makes his pitch. She's told me. She's sick of pushing her front door shut in their faces. Carol has her job in the gallery, and at the end of the day she's tired and wants to be looked after. What she likes is a man who can take her to just the right place for dinner, who can order well for her, who can make her talk and laugh. An older man, if you want, who can be leaned on a little.

Sure, we talked about getting married, and I really don't think I would have minded. That's the funny part of it; I can't say just what went wrong. I don't think it's the difference in our ages. I guess I'm what you'd call middle-aged, but not in any way that matters. I've seen too many of my friends get out of touch with things in the last thirty years to let that happen to me. I can remember back when I used to see all my friends in the same places almost every night. And then they stopped coming. Now I never see them any more. But I haven't let that happen to me. Right now, I can walk in anywhere and get a table — any place you mention. I see all the new plays and I know all the interesting people. Why, there isn't a columnist in town I'm not on good terms with, and they treat me fine. They've never written a nasty item about me yet. Sometimes I used to tell Carol these things, in a modest way, of course, but they just seemed to make her impatient. She was impatient about my job, too, and I think maybe our breaking up had as much to do with that as anything. She never wanted to know a thing about my work. I know that's fashionable with younger people nowadays — not caring about making money. But there was a time when being a broker wasn't a bad joke, the way it is now. I tried to tell Carol that, too. "What's funny about a broker?" I'd say. But she'd just give one of those woman's groans.

I'm putting that part down because this business started last fall, on the night Carol first got really sore at me. A Tuesday night, it was. I remember it was very early, no more than ten, when I took Carol home. We'd been in one of our favorite restaurants, but nothing had gone right all evening. Carol had run into some friends of hers, one of those earnest couples, and they'd spent the whole evening at our table talking about politics and Indians starving and some crazy new sculptor out on Long Island. That sort of talk just leaves me limp with boredom, and as far as I can see, it doesn't accomplish a thing except make everybody nervous and irritable. Carol always liked it, though, and it seems nowadays as if a person can't put in a friendly evening without talking about a lot of Cubans and Reds and getting all neurotic about them. Anyway, Carol was no ray of sunshine that night, and as we drove down Park in a cab she lit into me again for not saying anything all evening and drinking too much and being antisocial. *You* know. My God, me, Elliott Zachary, antisocial! But I didn't argue the point.

I don't think we said much of anything the rest of the way, but just before we got to Carol's place I tried to cheer her up a little. I said it was a damned shame that we hadn't kept Prohibition. I told her there used to be wonderful little places where a couple could go for a good dinner and some drinks and just have some friendly talk and a good, quiet evening together, but we had voted them out of existence.

But Carol didn't listen. While I talked, she kept humming to herself as she stared out the window of the cab. I can remember the side of her face and the way one earring reflected bits of light from the street lamps on each corner. When we got to her apartment, she said she was tired and she didn't want me to come in — no, not even for one last drink. I couldn't very well ask her what had gone wrong — not right on the street — so I just said good night and walked off. I think that was the first time we'd ever left each other without making some kind of a date.

Well, it was still early and I still needed a drink. I walked up Park, past all those new glass buildings they've put up that make it look like part of a world's fair or something. I wish they'd leave my town alone. I was feeling damned low and sorry for myself, and on Fifty-third I went into a place I hadn't been to in years, just on the chance I might meet somebody from the old days who could cheer me up. But the restaurant was jammed, like so many places now, and it seemed to be a brand-new bunch — lots of kids and people who looked like out-of-towners. I even had to wait a few minutes before I could squeeze in at the bar. I ordered a drink and asked the bartender if Alfredo was around, but he wasn't there — off in his place in the country, the barman said. Even the restaurant owners have to go to the country these days. I was looking around, trying to find somebody I knew, when right next to me at the bar I heard a man order a Bronx cocktail. I turned around and looked at him, because my God, I mean it had been a good twenty-five years since I'd heard anybody order *that* drink. And he was a young fellow, younger than I. But not as young, it turned out, as I thought at first.

He must have noticed that I was looking at him, because all of a sudden he asked me if he could buy me a drink. I was embarrassed about being caught giving the double-o, but he bought a round and we started talking. I had taken him for an out-of-towner, but no. Turned out he lived in the city. "I'm in the advertising game," he said. I said, "Oh, a gray flannel type," but he didn't smile. Then, just being friendly, I said, "Know any quiz programs you could get me on?" But I decided he was touchy about advertising, because he just looked at me in a funny way and said, "I beg your pardon?" So I laid off. I told him I was a broker, and he asked me if this wasn't a good time to buy railroad stocks, which I thought was his way of ribbing *me*. We had another round, and I asked him if he knew Alfredo. He said he did, and I told him there was a time when I could have walked into Alfredo's any day of the year and found at least three or four of my friends there — friends that knew how to take a quiet drink without yelling and doing tricks with the silverware and spilling ashes on the tablecloth and arguing about the United Nations. Then he handed me a surprise. He started talking about this town, about this town in the old days, and, believe me, he knew it. He remembered little speaks and dives and headwaiters' names that I hadn't thought of in thirty years. The very same places I'd been trying to tell Carol about. It bowled me over, because he didn't look old enough to have been around then. We had a fine time there talking, and I almost asked him how come I hadn't seen him around any of the spots recently. But I figured maybe he'd been broke. I ended up telling him a little about how Carol and I hadn't been hitting it off so well and how I wished I knew a quiet little place to take her to for a change — any place that wasn't jammed with kids. While I was telling him, he began to smile, and when I'd finished, he tipped down his drink, pointed his finger at me, and said, "I've got just the place for you. C'mon. I'll phone up Leon and tell him about you, and you'll be in."

Right there, I made my mistake, in thinking that this stranger could tell me about a place in town I didn't know of. I should have kissed him off and gone home; then I never would have gotten into all this business. But he acted so sure of himself that I said fine. We walked past all the crowded tables to the phone booth in back, where he stepped in and made his call. I had a funny feeling there while this fellow was phoning; I suddenly caught myself wondering if this hadn't happened to me years before, maybe right in this same room, with me standing beside the phone while somebody (not a stranger but somebody I had known in college) was making arrangements for us to get in somewhere else. Maybe that was why we used to go out so much; it used to be so much more trouble and more fun to get into a new place. Every night seemed different then, and we were all explorers. Then this man came out and handed me the receiver and I was talking to Leon. I felt like a hick, asking if there was any *possible* chance they could squeeze me in for dinner Friday night — just two of us. I felt like somebody in town for the first time. Leon said. "One moment, sir, while I speak to the boss," and left the phone off the hook. I guess the phone must have been in the bar, because there was an awful lot of talk and laughing going on. There was a girl right next to the phone talking very seriously, and I wish now I'd listened more carefully, to hear what she was saying. She sounded very young. But I could make out the tune somebody was playing on the piano; it was "Singin' in the Rain," very soft and slow. Then the man Leon came back to the phone and, yes, the boss said any friend of Mr. Cromartie's would be welcome, and he asked my name. I had to give it to him twice, because the first time he said, "Hold it a minute, will you? I can't hear anything in here when the cars go by." So I told him again, and I guess he must have known who I was, because he was very friendly.

Friend Cromartie was waiting for me at the bar and said he hoped everything had been O.K. Then he took out his wallet, pulled out one of his calling cards, and wrote the name and address of the place on the back. "I hope you can read it," he said when he handed me the card. "My friends keep telling me I write badly enough to enter that distinguished handwriting contest." But I know there's no mistake about the address he wrote, because I still have the card with me, with "Hugh Cromartie" engraved on it — nothing else — and on the back "Mr. Leon at Ray's" and then "117 West 46th Street" and a Longacre telephone number, written in his handwriting. I stuck the card in my pocket, we had another drink, and then I said good night and went home. All that time with him and you'd think I might have asked him once where he lived.

Next day, I woke up thinking about my screwy reservation, and I called Carol and said how's for Friday night in this funny place. I tried to tell her how I'd heard about it, but she was still giving me the freeze and it was no dice. Then, a couple of days later, who should call up but my sister Belle, just in from Cynwyd for a big weekend on the town. Belle always expects a free evening from me when she visits, so I told her we could try this new place I'd just heard about, and she said fine.

I don't know to this day whether Belle thought I was playing a trick on her, or what. But then I never have been able to figure out what she thinks about me. I picked her up at her hotel at eight, and she really looked quite pretty. Belle is always much nicer when she's away from that husband of hers. I gave the cabby the address Cromartie had given me, and I even began to think maybe it wouldn't turn out to be such a dull evening after all. But then we stopped in the middle of Forty-sixth, between Sixth and Seventh, and after I'd paid off the cab I turned around, and there we were in front of some big, modern building with a radio station in it, and Belle was looking sore.

I got out the card and checked the address again, but I'd told him right. There just wasn't any such place as Ray's — not that night, not at 117 West Forty-sixth. I was sore — sore at myself and at Cromartie — but I didn't even try to explain it to Belle, though she kept looking at me in that queer way sisters have, as if she thought I was losing my grip or something. We went up to the Plaza for dinner, and then Belle wanted to go on to a big night club, just like a real country girl. The evening got worse instead of better. The band gave me a headache and Belle just wouldn't go home until all hours.

I don't know what time it was that night when I suddenly sat up, completely awake and sober. I'd had a couple of aspirin and had been in a sort of sleep, but then I was awake and thinking about that restaurant and that Leon on the phone. I remembered how it had sounded listening to the noise in that place, how the girl had sounded talking, and I remembered, sitting straight up in bed in the middle of the night, what the man had said on the phone: "I can't hear anything in here when the cars go by." *What cars did he mean?* He hadn't been talking about traffic; automobiles don't make enough noise to bother a man on the telephone. My hands began to sweat, because I suddenly knew what Leon had heard while he was trying to get my name over the phone. It was a sound, a friendly sound, I had almost forgotten — a dull, heavy humming in the distance that grows louder and nearer until it bursts in on you with a roar of shaking steel and a bumping clatter of wheels, and although you aren't *listening* to it you stop talking, along with everybody else, until it goes out the other side of the room and goes rattling off, uptown or downtown, into silence. And I knew something more about Leon: he was brought up in this city, because only old-time New Yorkers ever said "the cars" when they were talking about the Elevated.

Then I turned on the light and found the card with the address — 177 West, all right. Between Sixth and Seventh. And the Sixth Avenue El has been down and forgotten for God knows how long. Fifteen, twenty years anyway. There was no point in doing anything about it in the middle of the night, but you can bet I stayed wide awake until morning. Jesse, the colored man who looks after me, almost fainted when I came out, dressed and shaved, at eight o'clock. I gave him Mr. Cromartie's card and told him to phone the number on the back and see if Mr. Leon or anybody was there. I had two cups of coffee while he tried to call the place, but finally he told me he couldn't get anything but a busy signal. I decided somebody must sleep there who left the phone off the hook until the place opened, so I took the card back and told him never mind. Then, just for the record, I went out and took a cab over to 117 *East*. There was no Ray's there, either, but I was sure Cromartie wouldn't have made a simple mistake like that. It wouldn't have made much difference, anyway, because the Third Avenue El is gone, too.

The minute I got to my office, I decided to phone Ray's again, and then, of course, I discovered what the trouble was. I even started dialing LOngacre 8098, but then I put the receiver down again with a sudden chilly feeling. There weren't enough numbers. There had to be an exchange number. After a while, I called the operator, and she told me I must want LOngacre 3- or LOngacre 4- or LOngacre 5-8098. But I had been ready to dial L-O-N, which is LOngacre 6 if you look at your phone. And there's no such exchange. There hadn't been an L-O-N exchange since 1930; I called the phone company and they told me the date. I tell you, I haven't been dumb about this.

Well, there you have it. At least, all that happened back there last fall, all the things I've been thinking about and wondering about ever since. And don't say it never happened. I'm a man who doesn't imagine things (you can't do that in my business), though I can tell you there have been some moments since last fall when I wondered about my-self. But I have Cromartie's card; I have it in my wallet this minute. Of course, Cromartie's the one I've been thinking about. How come none of my friends in the advertising business have ever heard of him? And, come to think of it, how long has it been since I've heard anyone say, "I'm in the advertising *game?*" People don't say that any more. And, finally, there's Cromartie's crack about his handwriting — "that distinguished handwriting contest." How did he re-member that, just in casual bar conversation? It took me a couple of days before I could pin that one down; it was the Marlboro cigarette handwriting contest — way back in the thirties, at least.

For a while, I thought Cromartie had played a joke on me. But then, why would he do that? It would be a bad joke, especially on a stranger. He had no reason to pull something like that on me. I decided I just had to find Cro-martie again. The very next week, I went back to Alfredo's, but even Alfredo himself didn't know anybody by that name, though Cromartie had said he knew Alfredo. He wasn't in the phone book; I called the one Cromartie listed, but they didn't know my friend. Then I began taking a drink in some of the old places — any place that had been in business since before repeal — hoping Cromartie would drop in. But nothing doing. I've even watched the obits.

I did one funny thing. I had that man so much on my mind, and the address and the phone number, that I even went back to Alfredo's again to make the phone call to Ray's. I just wondered if maybe on that one phone there Cromartie might have been able to get some screwy connection on a nonexistent number, God knows to where. But of course it didn't work — not for me.

I'm going out now to look for Cromartie again. I look for him every day. I don't know why, but I'm absolutely sure I'll find him, sooner or later. I thought I saw him the other evening on Madison, but he got into a cab before I could cross the street. But that's probably the way I'll find him — just meeting him on the street somewhere, or in an elevator. In a town like this, you're always running across the same people, so it's just a matter of time. I'll meet him, and this time I'll make him come with me to the place.

I keep wishing I had listened to that girl over the phone when she was talking. If I had listened, I could have heard what she was saying, I'm sure, because she was right by the phone. I've got the idea she's probably a thin girl, like all the girls then, looking even younger than she is, with her face hidden under one of those round cloche hats. Everybody seemed much younger then. She probably talks about all the regular things people talked about, and if I can meet her, I'll probably discover that she's very intense about them. I find I can remember them all very clearly, those old things people talked about then. Easy things, like Michael Arlen, and Grover Whalen, and Al Smith, and Lee Tracy in *Broadway*, and "Why do you drink those awful Orange Blossoms in a good speak like this?" Oh, I'd be able to get along all right. Evenings go very fast there, I'm sure, and chances are they end up just the way they used to: "Shall we go on to Mino's or Connie's Inn, or would you rather just go straight on home?"

Flight Through the Dark

I SHOULD have taken the train, Halleck thought. On the train, I would have slept. It's slower, but at least I would have gotten a little sleep. Now I'm going to be scared all the way. I'm always scared in a plane, and it's time I remembered and stayed the hell on the ground. He pulled his seat belt tighter and rubbed his sweaty palms together as the big plane shuddered and roared at the head of the runway and then lunged forward into the darkness. A minute later, they were climbing and banking, and Halleck looked down past the trembling metal edge of the wing and saw the lights of Washington and the dark shape of the Potomac below. There, he thought, that's where the plane must have hit, right at the edge of the water down there. Just before the landing and with all the people looking down, just like this, trying to make out a friend or a wife at the airport fence, glad that their trip was over, and wondering if they were going to be able to find a taxi. There had been no warning for them. Just the sudden, violent roar of the other plane and then the explosion and the falling. You probably never get a warning — All right! he said to himself sharply.

That's enough. Now, just cut it out. You're in a plane, that's all, and you're flying home. In an hour and a quarter, you'll be at LaGuardia; in three hours, with any luck, you'll be home. He relaxed his grip on the armrests of his seat and wearily rubbed his eyes with his fingertips while the engines muttered, "With any luck, with any luck." Christ, he thought, if only I'd gotten a little sleep last night!

Halleck had been in Washington for three days, talking to officials in the Commerce Department about materials shortages and new regulations that might be expected because of the continuing war in Korea, and compiling statistics and estimates for the export division of his company, of which he was a junior vice-president. The first evening, he had worked late in his hotel room, with a sandwich and a bottle of beer sent up for dinner. He had spent the last evening with his sister and brother-in-law, Agnes and Herb Jordan, in their three-room garden apartment in Georgetown. Herb Jordan was an engineer with Interior and had just received notice from the Navy that he was being called up again. They had talked late over highballs, and when Halleck got back to his hotel room, at twelve-thirty, he had gone to sleep instantly. Later, sometime in the dead of night, he had slowly, dazedly drifted up to the edge of consciousness. He was looking for something, something terribly important. Then, a second later, he was wide awake. He was on his hands and knees on the floor and directly under the open window of his hotel room, his extended hand sweeping in slow search across the roughness of the carpet. For a moment, in absolute astonishment, he had stayed there on the floor, with the cold winter air flowing over him, and the long curtains drifting and whispering about his head. Then he had turned on the light and looked slowly and carefully around the room for something he might have dropped or lost, something important enough to have called him from his warm bed and his sleep and set him to searching before an open window, nine stories above the street. When he had found nothing, he had begun to tremble, and then, in cold and sudden terror, had slammed down the window and bolted it and hastily dragged a big armchair across the room, tugging at it with his whole body until he got it turned around and jammed up against the window, its back out to form a barricade against the danger there.

After he had climbed back into bed and turned off the light, the trembling left him, but he could not sleep. He had never walked in his sleep before and he was afraid to go back to sleep. He lay there stiffly, smoking in the dark, while his mind scrabbled and rustled in the filthy leavings of fear. You weren't looking inside the room, it whispered. Your business wasn't there, was it? It was outside, out on the ledge there, and down in the street. You and all those others — the Cabinet officer and the statesman in Prague and the brilliant young lawyer in New York. Remember that professor, the one who taught you American literature? He took a room for it and left a note, neatly writing down, with a final touch of scholarship, what he had found out about himself. Is that what you were looking for — the note? Were you afraid it had blown away?

The plane droned and rocked in the night. Most of the passengers had gone to sleep. There wasn't any note,

Halleck said firmly to himself as he lit a cigarette. It was nothing like that. I'm awake now and I know it had nothing to do with the window. I just walked in my sleep, that's all. Maybe I heard something fall in the next room. Or perhaps it was just something I ate. I just felt uneasy, so I took a walk, and it frightened me. Six steps out of my little bed and I scared myself out of a night's sleep. A grown man of thirty-four, too. A father and breadwinner, a vice-president and a citizen of the atomic age. Former soldier, former adult. Let's see now: "Former adult, refined, afraid of heights, seeks correspondence with a kindred soul. Object, courage." That would bring me letters by the bagful! Everybody's scared now — scared in planes, scared in taxis, scared in strange hotel rooms. Everybody carries it around with him, and once in a while, usually in the middle of the night, he takes it out and looks at it. It only shows on some people, like Agnes. Halleck stubbed out his cigarette, thinking about his sister and remembering the evening he had just spent with her.

Agnes had always been a hard-luck girl. Three years older than Halleck, she had missed out on college, because there hadn't been enough money in the family to send her just then, not in 1931. When she had gone to work in a department store, she had fallen in love with a much older man, who was married and, it turned out, had no intention of ever getting a divorce and marrying her, although it took Agnes three years to find that out. When she finally did get married, it was, of course, to a hard-luck husband. Herb Jordan had just started to get ahead when the war came along, and then he had served five and a half years in the Navy without ever rising above the rank of lieutenant. Just as the war ended, he had got himself tied up with some salvage job at Okinawa that had kept him overseas until the winter of 1946, long after everyone else had come home. When Halleck had walked into the Jordans' apartment the night before, it hadn't surprised him at all to hear that Herb had been called up again. He could almost have predicted it. As the three of them sat and talked, Herb tried to joke about it. "One good thing about being a civil servant," he said. "At least I won't have to take a cut in pay. The Jordan family finances will not be imperiled. We'll still be able to afford meat loaf once a week."

Agnes, sitting stiffly upright on the day bed, a highball in her long fingers, didn't smile. "I am *not* going to be gay about this," she said stubbornly to Halleck. "I've told Herb that. I'm not going to be brave and cheerful and a gallant wife. Not again. I'm not going to move to Norfolk or San Diego and set up a hot plate in some God-damned hotel room, and I'm not going to travel across the country after my man in an all-night coach, and exchange confidences with some pimply nineteen-year-old girl about our husbands. I just *cannot* do it again. I'm not that young or that brave any more. And if Herb's office can't get him a deferment, then I'll just sit right here without him, and maybe I'll be able to come home at night and write lying letters again about how cheerful I am and how I know he'll be safe, and how the war — whatever war it is we're talking about — will be over soon. And maybe I won't even be able to do that. But I'm damned if I'll be gay about it." She gulped her drink, set it down, and stared defiantly out of dark, heavy eyes at her husband and her brother. A sudden tremor set the bracelets jingling on her thin wrists, and she looked down at her hands with surprise and clasped them tightly together.

If only she could have had a kid, Halleck had thought, watching his sister. Three kids and a big, handsome slob of a golf-playing husband in the banking business, with a house in Southampton and another on Mount Desert, and luck written all over him. He knew Agnes could never have a child, because Herb had told him, but Agnes had never mentioned it to him or to anyone that he knew of. She used to be so damned pretty, he had thought, and now look at her, there, in a dress four years old and her hands shaking.

Jordan stood up heavily and patted his wife on the shoulder before he picked up her empty glass and took it out to the kitchen. After he had gone, Agnes lit a cigarette and shook out the match as she looked at Halleck. "Anyway, Ben," she said, "you've got Lydia and the kids out of the city. I'm glad about that."

"What do you mean, glad?" he asked.

"What do you think I mean? Or don't you even talk about it yet? Even with the shelter signs going up in the streets and the magazines printing instructions?"

"Oh," he said stupidly, "that business. That's not why we moved out to the country. We just wanted to, that's all It's better for Julie and Tim, and it's easier for Lydia, not having to take them out to the Park all the time. It didn't have anything to do with the atomic bomb. Not that I know of."

"You don't think they'll use it?"

"Oh, hell, Agnes, *I* don't know. I don't think there'll be any bombs. Not right now, anyway."

Agnes shook her head slowly. "Insane," she said softly. "Insane optimism. That's what's wrong with all of us in this country. Looking for the bright side. Kid stuff."

"What should I do — move to Idaho? Build a lead-lined cellar in our house in Darien? Carry a Geiger counter?"

"No, just don't be so damned smart-alecky about it. Don't make jokes and don't go around acting as if you knew it was all going to turn out for best. It reminds me too much of 1938 and the way people talked then. Sitting back and making jokes and making plans and getting married and having children and saying all the time how Hitler was too smart to start a war."

Halleck had looked at the bitter lines around his sister's mouth. God, he had thought, she's really got it bad! I'll have to get her out of here and up to the country with us for a couple of weeks. This town is enough to throw anybody. "I didn't make any plans in 1938," he said easily, hoping she might smile. "I was too busy studying Vassar girls in 1938 to think about making plans."

Herb came back into the room, carrying three full glasses. "Cat's gone again," he said to Agnes. "And I can't find one of the kittens. That stupid animal's got no more motherhood in her than a guppy."

"Oh, *no!*" Agnes cried. She jumped up and hurried across the room and opened the door into the garden. "Here, kitty!" she called, stepping into the little back yard. "Here, kitty, kitty, kitty! Here, kitty! Oh, *please*, kitty-cat! Come, kitty!"

She's got a young girl's voice, Halleck had thought as he listened to Agnes calling and calling in the darkness. Her voice hasn't changed at all. She sounds just the way she did when she was a kid, back when we were all still at home and she used to sing in her bedroom. Every morning, she used to sing; she used to be mad about Russ Columbo. And he had felt a sudden wave of love and pity for the strange, too old woman who had once been his sister.

Agnes banged the door shut and ran into the kitchen. A moment later, she was back, with a tiny brown-and-white kitten struggling feebly in her hands. It eyes were still closed and there were gray blobs of dust clinging to its fur. "Oh, look!" Agnes cried. "Oh, look here! It was under the refrigerator, crawling around. It hasn't eaten. Its mother hasn't been near it for hours." She dropped on her knees and held the kitten out toward her husband with both hands. There were tears in her eyes. "Oh, darling!" she said. "What are we going to do about that cat? What are we going to do? What are we going to *do?*"

In the plane, a man seated directly in front of Halleck began talking in a loud voice to an Army officer in the next seat. "It's just like the good old days," he said. "Haven't seen the old town look so lively since '45." Halleck could see only the man's heavy pink cheek and the manicured nails on his gesturing hand. His voice was deep and confident. "Just as easy to do business there as during the war. Your boys in the Pentagon are glad to see a real businessman, for a change, now that they're on the spot again for tanks and machine tools. And another thing" — the man lowered his voice — "another way you call tell we're coming back to wartime is the Yids. Washington's full of Yids again, full of five-per-centers. You know what I mean? Just like the war."

Halleck grasped the arms of his chair again and concentrated on not listening to the man. Did you *hear* that, he said to himself. Oh, my God, did you hear that son of a bitch? For a moment, in his rage and trembling fatigue, he considered leaping up, shouting words, and then hitting the man from behind as he turned and half rose, surprise and injured dignity showing on his fat, smooth face. Slowly Halleck's anger subsided, leaving him chilly and close to tears. He looked out the window and saw a bright trail of sparks streaming from one of the engine exhausts, and, far below, the headlights of a solitary, hurrying automobile.

Agnes is right, he thought. Looking at it coldly, I have to admit she's right. Optimism is insane. After that little talk by my friend, here, after that brief, cheerful lecture on the status of the American capital and the American mind at mid-century, delivered by a well-informed, responsible citizen, a man of obvious experience and high connections, I must admit that I have been in the wrong camp. The hardy little army of optimists, still making plans, still raising families, still playing games, is about to lose one more member. My lines of supply are exhausted, my reserves are gone, and I'm going over to the other side. I am joining the sleepwalkers, the insomniacs, the tremblers, the window-ledge boys, and the movers-to-the-country. It's just a matter of time now, and I might as well be on the right side.

Bitterly, Halleck stared out into the rushing darkness while his mind busily picked at the latch on his little bag of thoughts, his own small store of familiar terrors. He remembered the time he had seen a dog maimed on the Merritt Parkway — the white-faced man, the dog's owner, climbing out of the parked station wagon, the little girl staring from the back seat, and the Airedale puppy dragging his smashed spine and useless hind legs behind him on the oil-streaked highway while the cars roared past. He remembered his college roommate, Pete Haskell, taking two years to die of cancer of the stomach. He remembered the photographs he had seen of the man who had been leading a horse along a street one morning in Hiroshima; there had been nothing left of them, but the image of man and horse had been blasted into the pavement like a permanent shadow, and you could make them out clearly in the photograph, the horse pulling a cart and the man still holding on to the bridle. And he remembered (he had seen them so often in his mind) the other scenes — the great buildings shifting and tottering on their foundations while dust and bits of glass streamed down from the high windows, and then, later, the families hiding in the woods, crouching under the trees, not daring to move or look up for fear that some tiny movement, some flicker of human life, might register in the delicate eye of an empty, mindless bulk hurtling through the sky, and so bring destruction down upon them.

At the airport, Halleck turned up his overcoat collar against a cold, whipping wind and ran down the steps from the plane. When he saw Lydia standing just inside the gate and waving to him, his stomach gave a great leap of fear. "What is it?" he said as he hurried up to her. "What's happened? What's wrong?"

"Nothing, silly," she said. "I just thought you'd like to be met and driven home this cold winter's evening. I thought I'd surprise you. I called up your office and they said they thought you had a ticket on this plane, so I took a chance. Betty Sullivan is sitting with the kids. Let's get out of this wind, shall we? I'm frozen stiff." Her hair was blowing around her face as she took his arm. "Aren't you glad to see me?" she asked. "Aren't you going to kiss me?"

When they got to their car, Halleck put his suitcase in the back seat. "You drive, will you?" he said. "I'm dead. I couldn't sleep last night."

Lydia climbed in beside him and fumbled in her purse for the keys. "I'm sorry, darling," she said. She started the car and backed out expertly. "Did you have a rotten time? Didn't the work go well? Didn't you get to see Agnes and Herb?" Before Halleck could answer, his wife said, "Oh, I forgot. I didn't know whether you wanted to eat in town or what, but I figured you'd been eating restaurant food for three days and you'd like to eat at home, for a change, so that's what we're doing. Is that O.K.? That way, you can see the children, too. They've been told they can wait up for you. Light me a cigarette, will you, Ben? I'm still frozen. The house has been down around sixty all day, so that thermostat must be broken again. You'll have to call that Mr.

What's-his-name in the morning. I've had a fire in the fire-place since before breakfast, so it hasn't been too bad in the living room. I've got on your old Army winter underwear, too." She giggled. "Wait till you see me."

As Halleck worked the cigarette lighter, he felt a resentful spurt of anger toward his wife. Listen to her, he thought. The weather and food and the house. She hasn't even taken time to let me answer her questions. Even if I told her about last night, she probably wouldn't hear me. The hell with it. I just won't tell her. He handed her the cigarette, and sat stiffly, looking straight ahead, as he remembered his fear and loneliness in the plane.

After they had come off the bridge and worked through the heavy traffic, Lydia drove faster. The concrete parkway made a regular clicking sound under the wheels, and inside the car it was warm from the heater. Halleck unbuttoned his overcoat and leaned his head back against the seat. Lydia had turned on the radio and was humming softly to herself. "That reminds me," she said at last. "You're going to get a concert when you get home. Julie has learned every word of 'Bloody Mary,' and she's going to sing it for you. She's been playing it on the phonograph every minute for the last three days, until I thought I'd go mad."

"Learned *what?*"

"You know, 'Bloody Mary.' From *South Pacific.* 'Bloody Mary is the girl I love.' "

"Good God! Flat, too, I bet."

"Yes, dear. Just like you — a tin ear. But she sings nice and loud."

"I can hardly wait."

Lydia laughed, and touched him lightly on the arm with her hand. "Oh, while I think of it," she said, "we're going to dinner with the McDermotts next week. Wednesday, I think. I just couldn't get out of it this time, they've asked us so often. I'm sorry. And we have a sort of half date for Sunday night. Helen called, and she and Don want us to go in to the hockey game at the Garden with them then. I said I didn't think we'd go, because we didn't like late nights Sunday, but I said I'd ask you first."

"No, let's not," said Halleck. "The Rangers are lousy this year anyway. How come Don and Helen are stepping out all of a sudden?"

"I guess I didn't tell you. Don got a raise last week — a big one, I guess — and they're celebrating it. Helen got a new dress. At Bergdorf's, yet."

"My!" he said softly.

"You'll probably see it tomorrow night. They're stopping in for a drink. Don wants to ask you what's a good place to buy a beagle. They've promised one to Patricia for her birthday and they want one just as good as our Sophie."

"If they'll wait till spring, they can have one of her pups. If that dog of the garageman's comes through this time. Personally, I think he's a nance."

Halleck turned and saw that his wife was smiling. Her face, dimly outlined in the light from the dashboard, looked extraordinarily pretty, and Halleck suddenly felt grateful to her for her familiar, cheerful expression, for the kindness and trusting humor of her conversation about plans and friends. Inside the warm car, he felt relaxed and far from danger, and he knew he would sleep this night. It wasn't much — a night's retreat into his own good fortune — but it was all he could see to count on, and, for the moment, at least, it was enough. "Come on," he said. "Step on it. I want to get home and see the kids."

The Poems

The Pastime

I. A KILLING

THE young man with steel-rimmed glasses walked into the dark hall of the apartment house and let the door close behind him. In a moment the clicking of the lock release stopped and he heard a door being opened two flights above him. A shrill feminine voice called down, "Who's that?" He stood still and said nothing. "Who's down there?" the voice cried, more insistently. Let her call, he thought. It was what Mr. Penney had said was one of the First Points of Approach. In a walkup you rang an upstairs bell but you didn't go up. No housewife would listen to you if you made her wait while you climbed two or three flights and her expecting God knows who — the TV repairman, perhaps, or the delicatessen or maybe even a boy friend. A salesman would just make her sore. Silently he put down his big case and listened to his breathing in the hall until he heard the upstairs door close. When his eyes became accustomed to the darkness, he carried his case over to a door on his right. He took off his hat and smoothed down his hair. He felt in his right overcoat pocket for the box containing the matched English military hairbrushes ("Our quickest seller and a fine opening line," Mr. Penney had said), but he didn't take it out. You didn't show what you had to sell at the door, but you had it handy. First establish your personality, then your merchandise. Pretending for a moment that the door in front of him was a mirror, he practiced his shy, polite smile — what Mr. Penney had called his "young America look." That was his own best First Point of Approach. He bent over and read the smudged typewritten card beside the door: "Foltz." Mrs. Foltz. All set. He pressed the doorbell.

Smiling, not touching the doorframe, he waited for almost thirty seconds. He was about to press the bell again when the door was thrown open by a woman. She wore a faded pink housecoat that bulged at the seams, and her plump face was powdered dead white. Her bleached hair was pinned in tight curls against her head. Without curiosity she leaned against the door jamb and looked at him with pale little eyes.

"Mrs. Foltz," he began hastily, "Mrs. Foltz, I trust I'm not disturbing you. I would consider myself an intruder if I were not convinced that I am here to help you. I am here because I know that you, like every American housewife, are interested in the latest and the best in modern accessories to ease work and strain in your home. My concern also is anxious to get your reaction to our line of personal accessories for the entire household. We have hairbrushes for your husband and children as well as the finest in hair and nail brushes for feminine allure." He paused for a mome t. The woman hadn't moved or spoken; she was still staring at him dully, or rather at the top of his head. Damn! It was all wrong. He should have mentioned brushes right away. Maybe she was a dummy or something.

"What is it?" she said abruptly. "What have you got?"

"Brushes," he said loudly. "Brushes, Madam." He fingered the box in his pocket and wondered whether he should begin again.

Just then there was a hoarse cry from inside the apartment. "Who's 'at? Who's your pal out there?"

Mrs. Foltz suddenly bent from the waist in a loud giggle of laughter. She straightened up, her hand over her mouth, and giggled louder. "My God!" she gasped. "My good, sweet God!" She turned from the open door and walked back into the apartment. She was still laughing. "It's the brush man," she whispered loudly. "The Fuller Brush man."

"Well, go ahead," the voice inside the apartment said. "Don't just stand there. Ask him in, give 'm a drink. I gotta see a Fuller Brush man. Don't let him stand out there in the cold hall with his brushes. Bring him in here."

Mrs. Foltz came back to the door, dabbing at her eyes with a tiny handkerchief. "C'mon in," she said, still giggling faintly. "Come in and sit down."

The young man picked up his case hastily and followed her into the apartment. This was a break, he thought, after a bad start. All the good sales were made inside; in the hall you didn't have a chance. He put his hat down on a chair inside the door and carried his case into the room. The place was small, and the air was thick with smoke and the smell of whiskey. Although it was still afternoon, the shades on the two windows had been drawn and a bridge lamp in the corner was lit. A woman was sitting on a small, flowered couch between the windows, and before her was a small table crowded with two whiskey bottles, a pitcher of water, an overflowing ashtray, and a huge glass bowl, almost an urn, half filled with potato chips. There were ashes and bits of potato chips on the floor. The woman was sitting carefully erect in one corner of the couch, a glass in her hand. Her wrinkled purple dress was pulled up over her knees and she wore a black velvet hat slightly askew. She looked about forty.

"This is Mrs. Kernochan," said Mrs. Foltz. "We were having a little drink here. Honey, this is the brush man."

"Sit down," said Mrs. Kernochan hoarsely. "Sit down there where I can see you. Take off your coat, Mr. Fuller."

"No, thank you," he said, smiling. He put his case down and sat uncomfortably in a little wooden chair under the bridge lamp. "I'll just keep it on, thanks."

"Lily, give Mr. Fuller a drink," said Mrs. Kernochan, squinting her eyes at him across the room.

"I am," said Mrs. Foltz. She poured some whiskey into a glass. "You like it neat or with water?"

"I don't think —"

"Oh, go ahead, go ahead," Mrs. Kernochan said. "We won't snitch on you, Mr. Fuller."

"All right, then," he said. "A small one with water."

"We haven't got no ice," said Mrs. Foltz. She walked over and handed him his drink. "We just ran out."

"So you're Mr. Fuller," Mrs. Kernochan said. "The original one and only. My God! Imagine you right here in the same room with me. How's business, Mr. Fuller?"

The young man smiled and glanced at Mrs. Foltz. "Well, you see, Madam," he said quickly, "I don't represent the Fuller people. They have their line and we have *ours*. Now, I don't like to knock a competitor, so I'll just say that we think we have about as fine an assortment of merchandise as you can find in the field. Now, if you'll let me show you . . ." He put his drink on the floor and knelt to open his case.

"The original one and only," repeated Mrs. Kernochan, peering at him.

"Honey, didn't you hear him?" asked Mrs. Foltz as she sat down on the other end of the couch. "He's not Mr. Fuller. He don't even work for them. He's Mr. . . ."

"Mr. Schumacher," the young man said, from the floor. He had his case open and was arranging brushes on the floor. "Mr. Linwood P. Schumacher." He looked up and smiled at Mrs. Foltz. "Now, Madam," he began, "here you see our complete line. A brush for every imaginable need. You will notice that they are ornamental as well as useful. The modern plastic bristles are —"

"Prince Hal!" cried Mrs. Kernochan from the couch. "My Prince Hal!" Mr. Schumacher started and almost upset his drink.

"Old Prince Hal," she repeated loudly. "Ah, you were the boy. Always in trouble. Always men on the bases. But how you could bear down! Prince Hal and King Carl! What a pair! You two and Fat Freddie. Those were the days, huh, Hal?"

Mr. Schumacher looked around wildly. For a moment he

seemed ready to bolt from the room. Then he saw that Mrs. Foltz was shaking with laughter.

"Ballplayers!" she gasped. "She always talks ballplayers when she gets like this. Ballplayers or babies. Today it's ballplayers. She thinks you're Hal Schumacher now. My God! Prince Hal!" She rocked back and forth on the couch, dabbing at her eyes.

"Hubbell, Schumacher, and Fitzsimmons," Mrs. Kernochan intoned, looking now at her glass. "Fitz on Saturday and you and Carl on the double-headers. Those were the days, huh? Remember 1933? Remember 1936, Schumie?"

"I'm afraid there's a misunderstanding," said Mr. Schumacher nervously. Still on his knees, he rummaged in his pocket for a card. "I'm Linwood P. Schumacher. No relation to the ballplayer, I'm afraid." He smiled up at Mrs. Foltz, but she was still laughing too hard to see him. "Prince Hal!" she repeated, almost speechless. "Always in trouble."

"You look different, Hal," said Mrs. Kernochan anxiously. She was squinting across the room at him again. "You look thinner. How's the soupbone, Schumie?"

"Well," he said slowly, "I did lose some weight last fall, when I had the flu, but it's coming back now."

"We've missed you, Hal," Mrs. Kernochan said, nodding her head. She downed her drink and unsteadily set the glass on the table. "We've all missed you. I remember when they said you were washed up. And what happened to the Giants then, Hal? What happened then? Who did they get? I'll tell you who. Mungo, that's who." She almost spat the name out. "Van Lingle Mungo. Just a refugee from Brooklyn."

She was silent, vaguely watching him as he began to put the brushes back in his case. Suddenly she groped on the couch beside her and found a pocketbook. Clutching it, she stood up, showering more pieces of potato chips on the floor.

"I'll take them," she said, looking into her purse. He could see the tears squeezing out of her eyes. "I'll take your dear, sweet brushes, Hal — every last one of them. You don't have to get on your knees, Schumie." She found some wadded bills and held them out to him blindly.

He had risen to his feet and stood in the middle of the room, looking from the money to Mrs. Foltz. Mrs. Foltz had stopped laughing. Now she laboriously stood up and walked over to the weeping Mrs. Kernochan.

"Now, wait a minute, Gloria," she said warningly. "This isn't Hal Schumacher and you know it. Hal Schumacher's doing O.K. for himself. And you don't need no brushes. Hal Schumacher isn't selling no brushes."

"Don't you do it!" cried Mrs. Kernochan. "Don't you stop me! Schumie was nothing in your life, Lily Foltz, but he'll always be my Prince Hal. And now look at him, with his brushes, the poor lamb!" She burst into a flood of tears, got up, pushed past Mrs. Foltz, and pressed the money into Mr. Schumacher's hand. "Take it, Hal," she sobbed. "Take it and have that chipped elbow operated on."

Mr. Schumacher looked over her shoulder at Mrs. Foltz. She looked at the weeping woman for a minute, then shrugged and turned back to the couch. "O.K.," she said. "Maybe it'll shut her up."

Hastily, Mr. Schumacher sat down on the chair and

pulled out his account book. On the printed slip he checked off the names of the brushes and added the figures up. He looked at the money in his hand and felt in his pocket for change. "There you are," he said, cheerfully. "Exactly thirty-seven fifty for the entire line." Then he ripped the receipt off, carried the case to the couch, and took out the brushes in handfuls. They made quite a pile beside Mrs. Foltz. He handed her the receipt and the change. "I'll just give it to you to hold, Mrs. Foltz," he said, talking fast. "Two dollars and a half makes forty. And thank *you!*"

"O.K.," said Mrs. Foltz. She stood up and walked out behind him. At the door he stopped and looked back, but Mrs. Kernochan had collapsed onto the little wooden chair and was sobbing quietly.

"I'm sure she'll find it useful," he said to Mrs. Foltz as he put on his hat. "We don't often sell the complete line to one person, but I'm sure she'll be satisfied. Of course, I don't usually sell samples, but with a big order like this at the end of the day I made an exception, just for your friend. Now with —"

"O.K., O.K.," said Mrs. Foltz quickly. "Just beat it now, Prince Hal, that's a good boy."

He went out and slammed the door behind him.

In the hall he put down his empty case — without the brushes it was very light — and lit a cigarette. Thirty-seven fifty! It was a killing, nothing less. Already he knew that Mr. Penney would mention it at the next sales meeting. Perhaps he might even be called on to give a little talk about it. As he picked up his case and started down the hall, he decided that it wouldn't do to tell about the liquor and the ballplayers. They might not understand. But no matter how you looked at it, it was a killing. "The initial resistance was high," he would say, "but once I got admittance and set up the display . . ." He began to whistle as he opened the outside door.

II. THE OLD MOXIE

IT was early afternoon. Outside, the hot midsummer sun was glaring white on Ninth Avenue, but it was cool and dark in the bar. A big fan spun slowly in the middle of the room, and pink clouds moved silently and mysteriously across the lighted glass panel of the jukebox beside the door. Dressed in identical blue linen play suits with flaring trouser legs, Mrs. Foltz and Mrs. Kernochan were sitting on the stools at the head of the bar. Mrs. Foltz, beside the wall, was reading the society pages, her newspaper held up and to one side so that the light from the street would fall on it. Next to her, Mrs. Kernochan stared moodily into her highball glass, one white, spike-heeled shoe hooked over a rung of her stool. Her streaked brown-and-gray hair was caught up with a pink ribbon tied in a huge bow over one ear. She paid no attention to the man on her right, who was leaning toward her, his right arm on the bar. His head almost touched hers as he talked anxiously.

"Honestly, Gloria," he said, speaking fast, "you'll like it for sure. It's just a little family get-together, you might say.

Just for my brother's birthday — he's goin' on fifty. He'll be there, and Dotty, his wife, and my kid brother, Gus. He's the one you never met, the one I told you about was the MP in Japan. All them, and four, five guys from my brother's office. I asked Dotty was it O.K. if you came, seein' it was just like the family, and she said sure, she liked you. She said you was a good sport and she liked you, Gloria."

The man's voice wavered and stopped. Mrs. Kernochan hadn't moved or looked at him. He stared pleadingly at her for a moment and then sat back on his stool with a sigh. There was a little silence.

"What do you know?" said Mrs. Foltz. "It says here the Marquesa de Portago just went back to Europe. I thought she was in Southampton. Last I read, she was in Southampton. Just last week she was there. Now she's gone to Paris, along with — wait a minute, now." She ran her finger down the page. "Oh, yeah. 'Woolworth heiress Mrs. James Donahue, Prince and Princess Alex Hohenlohe (Honeychile Wilder), Dick Cowell, the David McConnells (Julie Waterbury), Ileana Bulova, and John and Noreen Drexel. The departure of all these amusing people these past weeks has half-emptied our town and signals the onset of the dull, dull dog days in Gotham.' And then there's a picture here that says 'Society Beats the Heat' that shows a lot of people eating a picnic in one of those convertible Mercedes. At Meadowbrook, it says."

"Herman!" Mrs. Kernochan shouted suddenly.

The bartender came up from the far end of the bar, wiping his hands on his apron.

"You ready, Herman?" asked Mrs. Kernochan, smiling.

"I guess I'm ready, Mrs. K.," said Herman, putting his hands on the bar. "Not too tough, now. Nothing before 1930, remember."

"O.K.," Mrs. Kernochan said. "This is a pushover. Who played second base with the Giants, 1933 World Series?"

"Lemme see, now — 1933, hunh?" Herman looked over her head for a moment. "Oh, yeah. I think I got you this time, Mrs. K. You thought I'd say Burgess Whitehead, din you? Well, Hughie Critz played in 1933, din he? He was still up then, wasn't he?"

Mrs. Kernochan nodded her head sadly. "Hughie is right, Herman," she said. She pushed her empty glass across the bar toward him. "My round, Herman. That's three I owe you now. You must have been reading up, Herman."

"Naw," said Herman, pouring whiskey into a highball glass. "You know better than that, Mrs. K. Them record books is just for settling arguments. I don't read 'em none." He poured soda into the drink and put it down in front of Mrs. Kernochan. "How about you, Mr. Switzer?" he said to the man next to Mrs. Kernochan. "You want something now? A beer, maybe?"

"What?" said Mr. Switzer. "Oh, uh, no thanks, nothing for me right now." He watched Herman walk back down the bar and then turned quickly to Mrs. Kernochan again.

"Gloria," he said, his voice lower and more persuasive, "maybe you're thinking you won't fit in there next week. Because it's a family party. Well, if that's what you're thinking, Gloria, you're wrong. Like I said, Dotty said for you to come. And it isn't like we'd be there all night. I told you, after the party you and me could go out and have a drink, maybe. Maybe we could go to the Latin Quarter, like we did last year. You remember that, don't you, Gloria?" He was speaking faster and faster. "Remember you got all dressed up and how we had such a good time there? Last fall it was — last October. I remember it like it was yesterday."

Mrs. Foltz suddenly slapped her newspaper down on the bar with a bang. In the middle of the bar, a fat man with a cigar looked up at her. "Why don't you two lovebirds go somewhere else and argue?" she said loudly. "Why don't you get the hell out of here and let a person read his newspaper in peace? Why don't you run right over to the Latin Quarter this minute and spend the afternoon? You might get a front-row seat."

"I haven't said a word," murmured Mrs. Kernochan calmly. "I've been sitting right here with my yap shut all the time."

"Well, then, open your yap and talk to him," said Mrs. Foltz, going back to her paper. "Talk to him and maybe he'll go away."

"Me?" asked Mrs. Kernochan with dignity. "Me, talk to *him?* Don't be silly. I'm going to talk to Herman, my friend, my one true friend." She drained her drink and held the glass up in the air at arm's length until the bartender came up to her.

"Another, Mrs. K.?" he said anxiously. "I think you're rushin' me. You got me on the run."

"No, Herman," said Mrs. Kernochan, beaming. "I wouldn't rush you. Not you. Not my best friend. Just this one, Herman, and then I'm going to beat it. O.K.?"

"O.K.," said Herman. "Shoot."

"Same Series — 1933 Series. Gimme the Washington out-field."

"Now, wait a minute," said Herman, looking at the floor between his feet. "Just one minute. Nineteen thirty-three Senators. Outfield, hunh?" He straightened up suddenly. "O.K. Heinie Manush, Goose Goslin, and Sam Rice? Right?"

Mrs. Kernochan shook her head emphatically. "No, Her-man. Wrong. I got you one there. Manush, right, Goslin, right, but Rice, wrong. It was Schulte. Fred Schulte."

"You sure, Mrs. K.? You sure it wasn't Sam Rice out there? I saw one of them games in '33."

"Look it up, Herman." Mrs. Kernochan pushed her glass forward. "Look it up and pour me another. You and Sam Rice can pay for this one." She was smiling as she watched Herman go down the bar and pull a pile of worn *Official Baseball Guides* from a shelf under the counter. Then her smile faded and she dropped her eyes and began to draw designs with one finger in the circle of water her glass had left on the bar. "You know, Lily," she said slowly, "it isn't the same. Even the bets aren't hardly the same. Not with them gone."

"I know," said Mrs. Foltz. "Three years now, you been telling me."

"It seems more like a hundred years," Mrs. Kernochan said. "I can't get used to it. You know what they're playing up at the Polo Grounds now, Lily? Soccer, that's what! A foreign game. It don't seem fair."

"Look, Gloria," Mr. Switzer began again.

"They never asked me," Mrs. Kernochan went on. "They just up and left. They never asked was it O.K. with *me* if they went to the Coast."

"Well, you can follow them, can't you?" said Mrs. Foltz from deep inside her newspaper. "In the standings, I mean. And the box-scores. They're doing good right now, aren't they, now that Cepeda's hitting again?"

"Who's Cepeda?" said Mrs. Kernochan bitterly. "I never set eyes on him once in my life. He's not *real* to me. But Don Mueller was real to me. I can see him this minute, and the way he always stood with his neck so straight when he was at the plate. Whitey and Bobby were real to me. So was Sal. Even Wes Westrum. And they left me here all alone."

"You're not alone, Gloria," said Mr. Switzer eagerly. "I'm here, right beside you, and *I'm* real."

"Oh, for crying out loud!" said Mrs. Foltz disgustedly. She put down her paper, swung off the bar stool, and walked over to the jukebox. For the first time, Mrs. Kernochan turned and faced Mr. Switzer. He was thin and getting bald, and now his pale face was twisted into an unhappy smile. A watch chain was looped between the breast pocket and a buttonhole in the lapel of his wrinkled blue suit coat.

"How about changing the record, Al?" Mrs. Kernochan said, not unkindly. "How about a new tune, hunh?"

"But Gloria," he said, "you haven't told me nothing. You just sit there. How about the party and the Latin Quarter?"

"Al! Al!" Mrs. Kernochan said dramatically, shaking her head and looking away. "Al, you just ain't got it. You got no style, Al. You're always *asking* me. If you don't ask me, you gotta ask your brother's wife. Whyn't you just *do* something? Come around for me some night in your convertible Mercedes, Al. Come around some Sunday with a couple of tickets for Meadowbrook. Come in with a shiner some night, Al. Only, stop asking."

"But I haven't got no convertible Mercedes," Mr. Switzer said sadly.

"You haven't got a lot more than that, Al. You haven't got the big thing, the old moxie. You're pressing, Al. You're not loose in there."

"Moxie?" repeated Mr. Switzer desperately. "I'm not loose?"

Mrs. Kernochan looked at Herman as he came up with her drink, and shrugged. "You tell him, Herman," she said disgustedly. "I can't." She took a long swallow of her drink and put the glass back on the bar hastily. "Look," she said, turning to face Mr. Switzer again. "You ever hear of Ted Williams, Al?"

"Ted Williams? He's a baseball player, isn't he?"

"That's right, Al. A baseball player. 'A' for effort on that. Look, Al, Ted Williams has got it. Maybe he's almost washed up now, but he was always loose out there. Real loose. Even now when he gets in a game, he's playing like he'd rather be home in bed. He's so loose at the plate you think he's going to drop the bat, it's so heavy. Only, he doesn't drop it, Al. He pokes the ball over the fence, see? He's not pressing in there, Al. He's not worrying about his R.B.I., or who's ahead in the game, or whether he's going to get a seat at the Latin Quarter. See, Al?"

Mr. Switzer looked helplessly from Herman to Mrs.

Kernochan. "But, for God's sake, Gloria!" he said. "I'm not a ballplayer."

"O.K.," said Mrs. Kernochan firmly. "You're not a ballplayer. Look at somebody else, then. Look at Archie Moore. He's a fighter. Look at Willie Shoemaker. He's a jockey weighing like a hundred and five pounds. Look at . . ."

"Bing Crosby," Herman said.

"Sure. Look at Bing Crosby. You've seen him, Al. You remember about Bing. He's falling asleep in a chair, chewing a piece of gum and smoking a pipe, all at once. And at the same time he's singing something, a little ballad, for a record that's going to sell three million copies. He's got it, Al. He's loose."

Mrs. Foltz turned from her perusal of the jukebox titles and came up behind them. "Gloria," she said, putting a pudgy hand on Mrs. Kernochan's shoulder, "you going to go on telling all Ninth Avenue about Ted Williams's muscles or are you coming home with me while I wash my hair?"

"O.K.," said Mrs. Kernochan. "O.K." She finished her drink and took her pocketbook off the bar. "Three I owe you, Herman?" she asked. "Was I right about Schulte?"

"Schulte is right, Mrs. K.," said Herman.

After the women had left, Mr. Switzer sat without moving for a minute or two. Then he straightened up and beckoned to the bartender.

"Yes, Mr. Switzer," said Herman. "You want that beer now, maybe?"

"No, Herman," he said, talking fast. "What I wanted to

ask is — Well, I was just wondering if I could borrow a couple of them books for a while. Just for a couple of days. I'd bring them back to you, Herman."

"Books?" repeated Herman.

"Yes, them books you got under the bar. The record books. I think I'd like to see them."

Herman looked at him blankly for a moment. "I don't think . . ." he began. Then he turned and hurried down the bar. He came back with a pile of ten or twelve *Baseball Guides* and dumped them in front of Mr. Switzer. "Here," he said quickly, "you take them all, Mr. Switzer. Keep 'em as long as you like. You read up good."

He watched as Mr. Switzer stacked the books neatly and put them under his arm, picked up his Panama hat from the next stool, and put it firmly on his head. He watched him without moving as he walked out the door and started up the avenue.

"Hey!" said the fat man in the middle of the bar. "Hey, Herman! Hey, Ann Landers! How about another beer here? Or haven't you got the old moxie any more? Be loose, Herman, and draw me a beer."

"Shut up," said Herman as he picked up the empty glasses and walked slowly to the far end of the bar. "And don't call me no names."

"O.K.," said the fat man. "Maybe you're right. Maybe it isn't so funny, at that."

Summer in the Mountains

MEG PORTER had a look of determination on her face as she listened to her mother. Her eyes were fixed on her mother, and occasionally she raised her eyebrows or nodded slightly at a pause in the conversation, but her lips were clamped firmly together, as if to hold back any words she might later regret, as if no one could wring from her the mildest complaint or even a sigh of boredom or resignation. It was, nevertheless, a look of remarkable hostility, particularly from a woman of thirty whose face was normally pretty and animated. Both her husband and her mother had seen this look before; her mother, Mrs. Brockway, had, in fact, come to think it was her daughter's normal expression, and it worried her, but somehow she had never brought herself to speak of it. Larry Porter had once mentioned it to his wife. She ought to try, he had said, to appear happier and more interested when her mother was with them. She had no idea how bad it looked, he said, and Mrs. Brockway would think that that was the way her only daughter *felt* about her, which, of course, wasn't true. And besides, it made her look old. But Meg Porter somehow couldn't shake the habit. Now Larry, sitting across the room, tried to get her attention, to remind her again, but Meg wouldn't take her rigid stare away from her mother.

"And since Dr. Stout couldn't see me at any other time," Mrs. Brockway was saying, "naturally I had to call Mrs. Lincoln and tell her I wouldn't be able to come to the symphony after all. It was really a shame, because I do get out so little, you know. But the doctor had said to come back for a little checkup when I noticed that shortness of breath again, and Tuesday morning I just felt as if I couldn't take any air into my lungs. Of course, it wouldn't worry me if there were someone living with me in the hotel, but even with the elevator boys right outside that you told me I could call any time, it just isn't the same. I sometimes wonder what would happen if anything *did* happen to me and nobody there with me." Meg Porter opened her mouth suddenly and took a breath, but her mother held her hand up and smiled. "No," she said. "I know what both Dr. Stout and that other one said. I'm fine, perfectly fine, and there's really nothing to worry about. For my age. I'm not trying to scare you, Meg. I know you call up, and you know I love that. Nearly every day. And there's always the phone, in case anything . . . I really don't worry at all." She smiled bravely and shook her head. "It's just being alone, that's all. I'm afraid I'll never really be used to it. Of course, I don't have to tell you how much I appreciate — No, you told me not to use that word, didn't you?" She looked slyly at her daughter. "Well, how much I *love* that apartment and how glad I am knowing that it's mine, or almost mine. I always want you and Larry to know that I don't forget that or take it for granted. Ever. Well!" She smoothed her skirt carefully and then looked at Larry. "Where are you two going tonight?"

Larry Porter took his eyes off his wife. "It's just to cocktails with the Bradleys. You know — you met them here Christmas Eve. And then we thought we'd go to dinner at Luchow's. But we won't be late. Shouldn't be later than ten or so. Of course, we can always come back before then if you want to get home earlier. We could just pick up a hamburger."

"Don't be silly, Larry," Mrs. Brockway said. "I wouldn't dream of it. Jane and I always have a wonderful time together. You know I love looking after her. It's so much like the old days, with Meg. After her father died and before she went away to college. I'll bet she doesn't even remember how close we used to be."

"Of course I remember, Mother," Meg Porter said. She leaned forward and took a cigarette out of a box on the table beside her chair. "We used to play games. And we went to the theater. And —"

"And every summer to Chocorua," Mrs. Brockway said. "Larry, you have no idea how she used to adore it there. Sometimes I wonder how you all ever started going to the beach."

"Jane is crazy about the beach, Mother," Meg said. "She wouldn't go any place else. And neither would I."

"Of course, dear," Mrs. Brockway said gently. "It isn't the place that counts. It's just being with people that counts. People you love. I just hope, Meg, that you're *with* Jane enough. She's such a responsive little girl, and you have no idea how suddenly it all ends. Before you know it, she'll be grown up and off married to somebody, with a busy life of her own and lots of friends and parties. And then you'll start thinking back about your life and you'll remember every hour you had together."

"Mother, for heaven's sake! You don't honestly think that I neglect —"

"Oh, no, Meg," Mrs. Brockway said, smiling again. "I just mean that Jane responds so. I hope you appreciate it. Why, I always look forward to these evenings we have together. Jane and I have such fine times it makes me feel like a real member of the family, just for a few hours, while you and Larry have a good time by yourselves. What I mean is, really, that at my age you know enough to appreciate a little child. They just *give* themselves, the way grownups can't. Nobody really understands that until they're as old as I am and their own children have gone."

"Oh, *Moth*-er," Meg said, helplessly dropping her hands.

Larry Porter stood up quickly, looking at his watch. "We'd better go, darling. It's past five-thirty. I'll tell Jane we're leaving. I think she's in her room watching that damned kid show again."

In the cab, a few minutes later, Meg was almost crying. "Oh, God, darling," she said to her husband, "why is she so awful, and why am I so awful to her? I've just got so that I think that every word is a hint or a slam or something, and I just can't stand it any more. There ought to be a compatibility test for parents and grown-up children to take together, and if they fail, there would be a law that said they couldn't see each other or couldn't live in the same city together. No, I don't mean that, either. I don't *really* feel that way — it's too hateful. It's just that Mother gets me all mixed up."

"I know," Larry Porter said. He lit a cigarette and handed it to her. "You had that look again. You never look that way except when she's there."

"I know I did. I can feel it coming over me and I can't stop it. Every time before she comes, I say to myself, This time will be different, this time we'll really get along, and she won't talk about herself and how lonely she is and how dreadful I am. But then the minute I see her I know it's going to be just the same."

"It's not your fault, Meg," Larry said gently. "It's just that she's old. That and the money."

"I know it. But we can't help the money. She needs it, and we want to give it to her. But why does she have to be so damned *grateful?* I've told her not to do that. It just ruins everything, and somehow it makes me feel as if we weren't doing enough for her, either. We all know she couldn't live with us, even if we had room. She doesn't really want that — she'd loathe it. And I'd go absolutely crazy and so would you."

"I wouldn't allow it," Larry said. "I'll never get us trapped with that."

"But what *does* she want?" Meg almost shouted. "I call her up. I have lunch with her. I go to the movies with her. We have her for dinner. We have her in to sit with Jane, because I honestly think she likes it. We get the best doctors for her and try to persuade her that she really is as well as she can expect. Why does she keep talking at me, then? Why does she make me feel so damned ungrateful and mean?"

Larry stared out at the passing lights for a moment before he answered. "I think," he said finally, "it's just that she's old and afraid, and she wants somebody to share that with her. And nobody can do it. You can't share being old with anybody."

Meg turned in the seat and quickly took hold of her husband's arm. "Don't let me get that way, Larry," she said urgently. She squeezed his arm hard. "Promise me you'll do that, Larry. Don't ever let me get like that. Don't let me do that to Jane, ever."

In the apartment, after she and the little girl had eaten the supper she had cooked, Mrs. Brockway went to the living-room windows to draw the curtains. She felt tired, and there was a vague pain in her side. Before dinner, she and her granddaughter had played a game on the floor, throwing dice that sent little racing cars around a numbered course. She hadn't understood the game well and the floor had made her knees ache, but Jane had seemed excited and happy, and they had played it twice. Now she stood for a moment by the window and looked out at the darkness that meant that soon the little girl would have to go to bed. After that, after an hour or two, the Porters would be back. She would hear them laughing and talking as they came out of the elevator, and they would come in looking excited and happy, and Larry would offer her a drink, which she would refuse, and then it would be time for her to leave and go back to the barren hotel apartment, with the uncomfort-able bed, and the furniture that was not hers, and the steam heat that killed every plant she bought, and the silent tele-phone, and the strange voices in the hall late at night — all the ugly and frightening familiarities that had somehow become the place where she lived. There were a few of her possessions left there — the set of Thackeray of her hus-band's, and the Spode teacups, which she had to keep on the mantelpiece — but they no longer seemed like her own. Sitting there by herself in the evenings after she had turned off the loud, confusing television, she often studied these treasures of hers and tried to remember how they had looked back in her own apartment, the one she had shared with Meg — where in the bookcase the set of Thackeray had stood, and how the cups had looked among the other familiar china on the shelves in the dining room. But she could no longer remember. When her furniture had gone (Meg had pointed out that it would be foolish and expen-sive to keep up her old place or to store all her books and pictures and furniture), her remaining treasures had some-how lost their identity. Out of place and without com-panions, they had become exactly the same as everything else in her bare rooms — somebody else's belongings, which she was now expected to live with for a time.

It was this she tried to explain to her daughter when she came to Meg's house and saw it full of the warmth of lived-with and familiar objects: an album of records that Jane had left open on the floor, the dachshund's worn cushion beside the fireplace, the clamshell ashtrays, which the three of them had collected on the beach the summer before —

all the evidence of plans made long ago and happily accomplished. Seeing this after the cold emptiness of her own long afternoons, after the terrors of a sudden pain in the night with no one to call out to, Mrs. Brockway always wanted to tell her daughter what she had here in her home, to cry desperately to her, "You don't know! You're so lucky here and you don't know it. You can't know what it's like to be without it, when it's all forgotten, when your own belongings are gone, and your house empty, and there are no more plans." But somehow it never came out that way. When she tried (without complaining) to explain all this to Meg, it ended in a recital of her days, of what she had eaten and what the doctor had said. Meg always became impatient and angry, and Mrs. Brockway went away feeling ashamed, because she had said it all wrong.

"Grandma, look!"

The little girl had made a small tower out of the piled-up dice from the game, and now she sent one of the tiny racing cars crashing into it, knocking the dice onto the rug. "Bang!" she cried. "He hit the pylon on that turn and now he's out of the race. Dang! Dang! Dang! Here comes the ambulance!"

Mrs. Brockway sighed and closed the curtains. She would have to hurry. The little girl would have to be put to bed soon. There was less than an hour for the two of them to be together.

"Let's read now, Jane, shall we?" Mrs. Brockway said. "I'll sit on the couch and you can lie beside me, and we'll read anything you want. We'll have a nice, quiet time together, won't we, darling?"

"O.K.," Jane said. She dropped the racing car and ran over to the bookcase. "Here," she said, pulling out a book. "This one. Read me *The Tinder Box*, Grandma."

Smiling, Mrs. Brockway sat down on the sofa. Sometimes Jane was exactly the way her mother had been as a little girl. Like Meg, she was suggestible; at one moment she could appear frighteningly violent, but she could change her mood and her interest in a second. The similarity made the grandmother feel warm and happy. Now she took the book from the eight-year-old. "All right," she said comfortably, turning the pages. "*The Tinder Box* it is. I know that story. It has those wonderful dogs with the big eyes. Now you sit down beside me, and I'll start." The little girl quickly curled her legs on the sofa, and Mrs. Brockway put her arm around her, pulled her close, and began to read: "A soldier came marching along the highroad. One, two! One, two!"

As she read the familiar story, Mrs. Brockway kept glancing at the little girl's face, intent on the page. Looking at her, the grandmother felt calm. At these moments, she knew that the fears and pains of her hotel bedroom were not really part of her at all. She was the same as she had always been, capable of anything as long as there was someone near her whom she loved and could make happy. Meg could no longer accept that from her, but this little girl, her granddaughter, did. She knew Jane depended on her. All that was needed was for them to be together more often, not just for a few hours on an occasional evening.

When Mrs. Brockway finished the story, Jane didn't

move but kept staring at the page with an intent and abstracted expression. Suddenly, before the child sat up, before it was time for her to go to bed, Mrs. Brockway wanted to do something to preserve the moment, plan something that she could take back with her to her room, like a possession of her own — a guarantee of love and happiness to come.

She tightened her arm about her granddaughter. "Jane," she said softly, "how would you like to come and live with me for a little while? Just we two together. Wouldn't that be fun? We do have such nice, happy times together it would be fun to do it for a longer time. I know a lovely place we could go, perhaps in the summer, when your school is over and Mum and your father might like to take a little trip by themselves. Would you like that, Jane?"

"Where would Mum and Dad go?" Jane asked quietly.

"Oh, I don't know. Perhaps to Europe for a few weeks or on a motor trip somewhere in the summer. I haven't asked them, but perhaps, if you would like it, I could suggest it and they might think it was a good idea. They haven't been off by themselves for so long that they might say yes. And then you and I could go to the mountains together, to a place I know. I used to go there every single summer with your mother. We could get a lovely cottage, and there are mountains all around, all with long Indian names. And there's a lake, where you could learn to swim, right where your mother did. And you can climb mountains, and we could take little trips. Would you like that, Jane?"

"Could I have a bulldog?" Jane asked. "Jennifer French,

at the beach, has a bulldog, and Dad said maybe I could have one sometime — a dog of my very own. Could I have one in the mountains?"

"Well, maybe, Jane. It all depends." Mrs. Brockway gave her another little hug. "We'd have to see, but we certainly could try. Wouldn't it be fun?"

"Yes, Grandma," Jane said. She sat up and looked at Mrs. Brockway. "And we can take the bulldog to climb the mountains and take him to the lake, and he'll learn to swim with me, won't he?"

Mrs. Brockway laughed aloud; actually, the plan didn't seem impossible at all. They might do it this very summer. It wasn't too late. She would be very practical and write and ask about cottages first and then speak to Meg after she had heard, so that there could be no difficulties or arguments. It was the simplest thing in the world. A whole summer with Jane, every moment of the long months with someone she loved. She pulled the child close. "We'll make a little secret of this, Jane, won't we? You won't tell Mum tomorrow, and then we'll talk to her about it together some day soon and surprise her, and she'll be so glad you can go to the mountains just the way she did."

"Not tell Mum?" Jane said doubtfully.

"Not right away, darling. It'll be a surprise, see? And then when we do tell her, you can explain how very much you want to go and spend the whole summer with Grandma. And after that, who knows? Perhaps we can do it again and we can stay even longer together. And we could go for a little trip next Christmas, just the two of us, on the train. Oh, you'll see! We'll have fine times together, and we'll have a lot of them!"

Mrs. Brockway had been hugging the child close to her for a long time, and now Jane began to struggle under her arm. She pulled herself away and stood up, and Mrs. Brockway was astonished to see that there were tears in her eyes.

"Go away for *Christmas?*" Jane said in a frightened voice. "Where will Mum and Dad be? Won't they be here for Christmas?"

Mrs. Brockway was frightened now, too. "Of course, darling," she said quickly, putting her hands out toward the child. "Of course they will. You don't have to go away for Christmas if you don't want to." She hadn't meant to go so far with her talk and plans. All that could come later. She caught Jane's hand and pulled her back to the couch. "You don't have to go anywhere, Jane," she said, trying to make her voice warm and soothing again. "Just to the mountains. Just this summer in the mountains, darling. You and I together."

But Jane roughly jerked her arm free and took three quick and defiant backward steps away from her. Mrs. Brockway again reached her hands out toward her granddaughter, and as she searched hopelessly for the words to recapture what she had lost, she suddenly thought she saw on the red, tear-streaked face of the little girl a flicker of expression she had noticed before in the eyes of the young and the strong — a bright, animal look of rejection and fear.

My Own Master

I DON'T remember how I ever got into this line of work. I think I used to like it, but now I don't care for it at all. With all the many years I've been at it — and believe me, it's been a long time now — you'd think I would have come to detest it before this. I've always known some of the bad sides to this — this *career* I have, but they're the easy ones, the drawbacks you'd spot right away. Insecurity, dubious future, long spells of an idleness for which there is no cure, and then sudden hazards and furious excitements and passionate ardors, sometimes all in the space of minutes. These to name but a few. It's no work for the weak or the cautious. But that's not what troubles me. I learned about all those way back when I was a beginner, and I've come to expect them; I travel very light, I'm light on my toes and easy with my attachments, and I'm usually ready to move on at an instant's notice. I'm quick — there's no denying it. No, what afflicts me now is something I've only begun to sense, and my deep trouble is that I can't say precisely what it is. Being so smart and sharp and experienced, it embarrasses me to have to admit to an ignorance, to something

I hate not knowing. But it's there; I feel it like a wind in my face. Maybe if I write about it now, between jobs, it will become clear to me. But I'm not sure.

Don't get the idea that my work is dull or *all* bad. My last appointment, for instance, was a good one — in some ways, the best I can remember. My employer, Rennie, was a steady fellow, a joy to be with, and not too extravagant in his demands. Nothing like that creature in the West of this country who kept me crashing about in cold, heavy armor the entire time I was with him. Or the one whose pleasure it was to send me racketing about the countryside in those tremendous racing cars he'd invented — Voom-*voom!* — and who then, like as not, would make me drive smack into the side of the garage or halfway up a tree in the driveway. Rennie was a quieter kind, and more thoughtful. If he fired me off in a rocket, it was only for short flights; he wouldn't keep me up there, forgotten, for weeks at a time, like some I could name. At the same time, he wasn't too conservative. (If there's anything I detest, it's tea parties and trying to make conversation with a lot of idiot dolls.) Then, too, there were no brothers or sisters to horn in on us or laugh at me, and no dogs or cats for me to fight. I guess it was just about perfect for me at Rennie's. It's sad to think of its being over.

I went to work there last year in the fall, just after the family had moved into a new apartment. New for them, but not *new.* I don't know what the man did for a living, but I think it was selling something; he used to be gone for two or three nights during the week. The wife was younger than he was, and I guess she was pretty. At least, Rennie told me she was pretty, but I don't know; I don't have much to do with the grown ones and I don't like to think about them if I can help it. They don't care for me, so why should I care for them? (I've been employed by some of them, of course — very old, most of them — but it's dull work. The last assignment like that I had with a Mr. Armbruster, who was ninety-two years old and in the hospital, and I was never so bored in all my life. It was a short job, but all I did that whole time was to sit at the foot of his bed and count out money for him: ". . . seven thousand, eight thousand, nine thousand, *ten* thousand dollars, Mr. Armbruster! Oh, and here's another five thousand you've just made, sir.")

There is trouble in most houses, and Rennie's was no exception. From what I could learn, I think they'd come down in the world. The apartment wasn't as good as the one they'd just left. One Sunday morning, they left their bedroom door a little bit open, and from the conversation I picked up I gather that something had been the man's fault. He was talking fast and very high up: "I know, I know, I know! You told me it was a bad idea and wouldn't work, and I went ahead just the same. You were right and I was wrong, but for God's sake be *quiet* about it for a change!" There was a long silence, in which you could hear him tramping around, back and forth, and then, sort of snuffly and half covered in the pillow, she said, "That isn't what I mean. You know I'm not like that, Lou. I only want things to change. I want us to get out of here, and I don't see how we ever will." From that, I think the man had made some kind of mistake that had cost them a lot of money, and they'd been forced into a poorer life. Certainly the apartment wasn't much. The view from Rennie's window was onto an air shaft, the couch in the lobby downstairs had an old salmon-colored slipcover that was all frayed along the bottom, and the elevator man wore slippers on the job and always had a half-smoked cigarette sticking out from under the edge of his cap. But I've seen worse places. At least Rennie had a room of his own, and that was where he and I spent so much of our time together.

It was a standard kind of operation at the beginning — a few minutes on, then a day or two off. I was always changing then. Sometimes I'd come in with my fireman's helmet on, or in my old lion's suit, and then the next time he'd have me in business clothes, like his father. There was a stretch when I thought I was going to end up being nothing but a general, all medals and guns. But then Rennie and I began to talk, sometimes an hour or more at a time, there in his room, and he found out what pleasure we could have together. After that, I was just me — no costumes. He'd have me there every day.

What did we talk about? Almost everything, in the end. Knowing my place, I always allow my employer to start conversations, but then I'm a great help. For one thing, I always understand, I always agree. "Don't" and "must not" aren't in me. And I'm an adventurer at heart, ready for anything. On a typical afternoon, Rennie and I might spend a while driving buffalo herds, riding bareback in feathers and shooting off our rifles, and then, liking that, we would enlarge our stock to include some gazelles, very tall and with great horns, and a few zebras and large red dogs, and after making camp and starting a fire, we'd pick out one of the dogs and win its favor with some choice scraps of buffalo steak, and then we'd name it, and it would become our devoted companion and would sleep just outside our tent at night, keeping watch against snakes and other creatures of the darkness. Or, by contrast, we would make plans for a boy named Philip, who was in kindergarten class with Rennie, in the mornings. Philip was an extremely large boy, Rennie said, with strong hands and a fat, white face. We buried him up to his waist on a sand bar, and then an ocean liner, adrift in a storm, beached itself right where Philip happened to be, and its huge iron bow drove him thirty feet straight down into the sand.

Our best time together was after lunch, when Rennie was in his room to be quiet. If we were talking, he liked me to stand on a bedpost. Often, though, he'd set me to doing things to amuse him, and he'd just lie on his bed and watch. They were the ordinary things everybody likes — walking up one wall, across the ceiling, and down the other, or taking flying leaps onto a windowsill across the air shaft, or growing until I was taller than the top of the closet door. All those are old stuff to me, but I didn't mind doing them for Rennie, he took such joy in them. I couldn't always please him, though. I was no good at being like his father, for one thing; I couldn't make out what he wanted from me then. I made up for it in other ways. You'll remember that I said I was quick. Well, one day the two of us were working together on a painting — a seascape painted on a page of an old evening newspaper — when a large blob of paint landed on one of Rennie's shoes; it looked so interesting there that I suggested that he go ahead and finish the job. He was just putting on the last pretty touches of green around the heel when his mother came in. I heard her at the last moment, so I whipped under the bed. I could hear the whole unpleasant business from there, and I could see her angry feet as she moved around — putting Rennie to bed for punishment, throwing away the painting, throwing away the two perfectly good jars of paint, wiping up all the trickles on the old rug, and drawing the shade. Rennie didn't say a word, but just as the mother was going out, carrying the shoe and leaving the room all full of discouragement, I made a lightning-fast sortie from my hiding place, bit the woman right in the behind, and was back out of sight in an instant. I heard Rennie laugh, and I was sorry about what happened to him then, but he told me later that it had been fully worth the price.

I could go on about me and Rennie, but you get the idea. The times we had!

Rennie's mother found out about me quite soon; they almost always do. He began to invite me out in the afternoons with them — I never went to his school — and she heard us talking. The father's turn came one Sunday, at lunch. Rennie had brought an extra plate and fork for me, which he put just to the right of his place. He had transferred a bit of mashed potato to my plate and was whispering something to me, when the old man saw him and stopped his chewing. "What's this?" he said in his half-annoyed sort of voice. (I disappeared under the table at this point. I had *told* Rennie that this mixing with the grown ones was never a good idea, but he had his own way about it.)

"Haven't you heard?" the mother said. "We have a new boarder. He's Rennie's friend."

"I don't see anybody," said the father.

"Well, he's here," she said, in a patronizing sort of way. "His name is Chuck." (This will show you what I mean about adults. My name with Rennie was *Juck*, except for the times when I was The French Man, and she never did get it straight.)

"What is he — a Teddy bear, or something?" he said, chewing again.

"I don't think so," the mother said. "I think he's another boy, about Rennie's age. Or maybe a man."

"What is he, Rennie?" he asked. "Man or beast? Or figment?"

"He's gone," said Rennie.

"Didn't he like his mashed potato?" the father went on, clashing his knife and fork. "Perhaps he'd prefer a Martini. What do you think?"

"He's gone," said Rennie again.

"Well, bring him back. I want to see him. Can *you* see him?"

Rennie didn't say anything, and after a moment the father said to her, not joking at all, "Now he's stubborn again."

"Well, it's *his* friend," she said.

He uncrossed his legs and put his great feet flat on the floor. "Aw, do we have to have this, Liz?" he said. "I'm tired on the weekends. The child won't talk, and he's begun seeing things, and you stick up for him."

"It's perfectly normal," she said. "I looked it up in the book. They often do it at this age, particularly single children. It's just a phase."

"Well, why doesn't he have real friends, like other boys? Why doesn't he do things like other boys? Play ball, or something. This just isn't healthy."

"Oh, come on, Lou," she said, pleading. "It's fun for him. Didn't you ever have a friend like that when you were young?"

"I did not," he said. "Thank God. I was with my real friends, doing real things."

"Well, it just happens we don't have many real friends right now. Rennie, or you and me, either. We're in a new neighborhood, and Rennie doesn't know anybody well yet. He's shy." She was getting upset. "Give us time, will you? And while we're talking about this, why don't *you* do something real with the boy for once? You're away half the time, and when you're here you hardly talk to him. You've forgotten how to enjoy things, Lou."

"I do things with him," he said stubbornly. "I took him down to the Battery just a couple of weeks ago. We had a good time, didn't we, Rennie?"

There was a silence.

"Didn't we, Rennie?" the man repeated dangerously.

"We had a good time," Rennie said. He sounded like a machine.

The man's napkin came flying down onto the floor, and

his chair was pushed back. "I'll take my coffee out here," he said, and he walked out of the dining niche and into the little living room. There was a click: him turning on the television.

"If you want coffee, you'll just get it yourself!" she called out.

And that was the end of lunch. That afternoon, Rennie and I made one of our longest and finest journeys together. We took a ferry from the Battery, traveled north at great speed, and shot dozens of polar bear. Their blood showed up beautifully on the cold white ice. There were just the two of us, which is the way I like expeditions. And then that night, after he'd gone to bed, Rennie set me to spying on his family for the first time. He instructed me to watch them while he slept, and to report my findings to him in the morning.

I must be the finest spy in the world. I know all the tricks of keyhole and closet; I can stand motionless for hours behind a drawn curtain, listening; I can work myself so cunningly into the design of a wallpaper that a person can sweep his eyes over me a hundred times and not suspect I am there. But I know something even more important — the key rule for the master spy: *Only tell your employer what he wants to hear.* Grown people almost never tell the truth, anyway.

That first night of my watching the parents, I stationed myself behind the bottles in the part of the bookcase they'd made into a bar, and I heard everything they said. It was dull talk — no excitement, no raised voices. Mostly they talked about money and about the time ahead. They agreed that, with luck, they might be able to move again in another year, this time to a house somewhere outside the city. The man would look for another job when he could, one that would keep him at home more. They would do better by the boy. Lies, lies, lies! The man even said he would try not to be annoyed by me. (I had to cover my mouth to keep from laughing out loud. I knew *his* kind.) They didn't say anything about that delightful scene at lunch, which disappointed me. But that's the way Sunday nights often are; the grown ones are quieter then, and I've noticed that it's their favorite time for fooling themselves about the future. Anyway, I knew that none of this would interest Rennie in the slightest, so in the morning I told him that his father was going to be off on trips and out of Rennie's way a great deal more of the time but that he would come back in the spring and all of us would go off to a lovely beach and live in a big house together for the entire summer. I even added something about a promise of a real puppy for Rennie for Christmas; maybe I even said two or three puppies. Rennie was delighted with my report, of course, just as I had known he would be.

The days slipped along, autumn and then winter, all much as before. Mornings, I waited, dead-bored and half alive, while Rennie was off at his damned school, and then the afternoons were ours — sometimes wild and funny, sometimes sleepy and secretive — until the mother came to take him outdoors. I went along with them some days, a cap pulled low on my head, and the master and I would consult pigeons we knew or draw maps of the underground with chalk — tunnels and gun emplacements and that sort of thing. Evenings when the man was home, I'd spy. Now and again, Rennie brought a friend home for the afternoon — it was his mother's doing, of course — and I'd have the whole long day off. Actually, Rennie did call me in a couple of times to introduce me to a schoolmate, but it didn't work. The intruder would begin to cut up rough with me, or even try to steal me, and there would be tears. I didn't care; tears are good luck for me. Christmas came and went — no puppy, of course, but a slow time for me just the same — but then the weather went bad and there were better days for the two of us, all indoors. Times when Rennie was in bed with a cold were the best of all. Oh, how devoted, how loyal, how demanding that young person was! I can scarcely remember any master who has asked more of me. But I gave him full measure and was happy for it. Intense — that's the way we were together. I should have realized it was too good to last.

They tried to break us up, of course. I'd hear them conspiring at it after dinner. Later, acting on plan, the mother would try to invite me to the table for weekday lunches ("Shall we set a place for Chuck, Rennie?" . . . "Is Chuck hungry today, do you think, Rennie?"), but Rennie knew better than that by then. And, once in a while, the man would make a big try for Rennie on a Saturday afternoon — a movie, or reading aloud, or a tiring afternoon of sledding on the wet snow in the park. I didn't worry much about those. They were spurts, special efforts. I was sure that the man was a fake in the long run.

They were persistent, though. I've got to hand it to them.

They kept at it, in their dreary way. Those two were talking together more and more in the evenings, all laughs and looks across the room; it was sickening to watch. Even their silences were different; there was no more edge to them, no delicious feeling that one ill-chosen word could fall between them like a smashed vase. I was uneasy, and I tried to listen to them even on nights when Rennie had forgotten to put me on post. Also, I had troubles of my own; I was getting tired. That always happens to me on these full-time, exciting assignments, and I hate myself for it. I began to feel myself getting dull and vague, sometimes even when Rennie and I were alone together. I had begun to exhaust myself. One day I suggested another undersea voyage, the third one that week, and Rennie was disgusted with me. "Go away, Juck," he said, punishing me. "You damned old man." He was right. I was feeling confused and foolish, a thousand years old. And Rennie hurt me in other ways. Sometimes he and the other two would go out together on a Saturday or a Sunday, and when they came back Rennie would keep the day a secret from me. He'd call me out at night and look at me, and then he'd smile and say nothing about where they'd gone or what they'd done. He could be that cruel.

Then March came, and I suddenly took hope again. For one thing, the money trouble had returned. The man was away for longer stretches, sometimes five whole days in a row, and when he came home he'd look angry and hopeless. There were hard words in the evenings again, and the woman sniffling in the bedroom, and Rennie set me to listening and watching almost every night. One evening, they had one of those long grown-up arguments about a perfectly ridiculous thing. One of the old chairs in the living room had got its arm broken, so that it hung away at an angle, and they started in on *that*, as if it were something really important. I was watching from a perch on one of the slats in the Venetian blind; I could see her reddish, dark-blond hair just below me to my right, and, on the other side, the thin place on the top of his head, and the backs of his big hands that kept lighting cigarettes and jabbing them out as they argued. She said the chair had to be replaced or at least fixed right away, because they couldn't have anybody to the apartment with it looking like that, and *he* said it was just impossible, they couldn't do anything about it with their money the way it was then. So they went at it, back and forth and louder and louder, until my head was turning like somebody in the grandstand at a tennis match and I was kicking my heels with pleasure. Then I heard Rennie calling me, and I went in to him, trying to hide my grin, and told him it was only a television movie, all wars and shooting, that had waked him up, and that I'd see to it that his parents would never let it happen again.

Then, right in the middle of this time, a rainy Sunday afternoon came along. Rennie was still being careless, almost offhand with me; he had me right in the living room with the other two that day, almost as if he was looking for trouble. They were reading the papers, and Rennie and I were playing a very complicated game with a deck of cards in the middle of the floor. Rennie had beaten me the first two hands, 100-0 and 700-2, and we were scattering the cards around and talking in low voices while we got ready for the third, when suddenly the man got down on his hands and knees and started picking up the cards. "Come on, Rennie," he said. "I'll teach you a real game. I'll show you how to play Old Maid." It took him a long time to explain about suits and matching and the names of the cards, and Rennie kept getting mixed up and dropping his cards. I just sat there, out of it. They struggled along, and after about ten miserable minutes the man said, "Well, Ren, don't you think this is more fun than playing silly with that Chuck?"

Rennie didn't say anything, and the man said, "What about it, Rennie?" (He never knew when to let something alone.)

Rennie sneaked a look at him and then, turning his head away but all nerve, he said, "No. I don't like this game."

The man put his cards down. "Is he here, Rennie?" he asked. "Is Chuck in this room?"

"That's not his name," Rennie said.

"Is he in this room, I asked you."

"He's around," said Rennie.

"Lou," said the mother from her chair, "remember what we decided."

"I'm sick of this," he said, getting up. "I'm going to settle this once and for all." He went out into the hall and came back with a rolled-up umbrella in his hand. "Where is he, Rennie?" he said. "Where's Chuck?"

"I don't know," Rennie said, watching him carefully. He could see me perfectly well, right beside him.

"Is he *here?*" he said, pointing to the floor about a foot away from me. He raised the umbrella and brought it down *bang!* on the floor. Rennie and I both began to laugh.

"No?" the man said, half smiling but with his face be-

ginning to flush. "Then what about *here*, or *here*, or *here?*"
Bang! he hit the floor again, on the other side of Rennie,
and *bang!* behind him, and *whup!* on the cushion of the
broken chair. Rennie began to shout with excitement as his
father went around the room slashing and jabbing and cutting with the umbrella, like a swordsman gone mad. I sat
where I was, safe as safe. I'd never seen such a sight.

"He isn't here, is he, Rennie?" shouted the man, still
knocking dust out of the curtains and sofa pillows. "He
isn't here, because he isn't real! Isn't that right, Rennie?
Chuck isn't real, is he, Rennie? Answer me!"

Rennie's shouts suddenly turned to wails, and tears burst
out of him. He was afraid, and no wonder; even my own
heart was thumping a bit. He scrambled to his feet and ran
into his room. The woman said, "I could kill you, Lou,"
and followed Rennie, and after a few minutes I stood up,
too, and coolly brushed the dust from my clothes while I
looked at my ridiculous adversary, who was still panting
and muttering to himself in the empty room, and then I
followed the procession. I hadn't lifted a hand, but I felt as
if I had just won a battle bigger than Trafalgar.

I waited just outside the bedroom door until the mother
came out. My master was lying on his face in bed, on top
of the covers, sobbing softly. He looked lovely there, my
pretty young boy in trouble; the backs of his bare legs
seemed to shine in the half dark of the room. I crept up
beside him on the bed. There were fine golden hairs growing up his neck, just below the hairline; I had never noticed
them before. "I'm here, Rennie," I whispered into his ear.
I was smiling to myself. "He didn't frighten *me*," I said.

"I'm here with you always, Rennie, my friend." Oh, I was fond of him! I felt we had never been so close, so safe.

Now comes the part of my story that is difficult to tell, for here I become lost. I was certain I had won Rennie that day, and that we would be together for months and years to come. I couldn't have been more stupid, more mistaken. My magnificent victory turned out to be only their last defeat; after that wet day in March, my exile was assured. Was it my fault somehow? I'll never know. I don't understand families.

I see that I have said almost nothing here about the woman, Rennie's mother, and I now think I know why. She was my adversary, really — not the man. She was the one who ended my stay with them. I have said that perhaps she was pretty, and I know she was gentle, but there was more to it than that. There was something else — a look about her that I couldn't penetrate. I've known mothers in my time, of course, and most of them were nothing like this woman. That look meant something between her and Rennie; it was a signal of some kind. Even in the best of times, back when Rennie and I were inseparable, it would happen. He and I would be planning or adventuring, with the door of his room open, and she would come by in the hall, carrying something or busy on some dull grown-up errand. She'd look in as she went by, not stopping, and Rennie's gaze would flick toward her. Just in that instant, he would abandon me, leaving me alone on a mountain trail or in the dusty cow-town we were subduing. The moment would pass and he'd return to me, but while it lasted I felt death in me. There was that much in her look; it was a promise to him of what the other world, their world, would be to him.

She was the one who turned my triumph against me. It happened the same day, at supper that Sunday night. Rennie brought me to the table — to celebrate our renewed friendship, I thought, and to rub it in a little. As you might expect, it promised to be a nice gloomy occasion. Nobody said much for the first ten minutes, and Rennie was arranging his peas into dotted lines instead of eating them. The man was trying to look firm and unconcerned, the way men do when they know they've been foolish. Then I noticed Rennie watching his mother in an almost frightened way. I looked and saw that she had put down her fork and was bending her head over her plate. Her shoulders were shaking. Then she straightened up suddenly and let out this appalling screech of laughter. "Oh, my *Lord!*" she cried. "I shall never forget it! 'Is he *here,* Rennie?' 'Did I get him yet, Rennie?' Bang, crash with that crazy old umbrella! The Count of Monte Cristo — fighting Rennie's — Rennie's little friend!" She was laughing so hard by now that the words were coming out in gulps. "It was an *awful* thing to do, Lou, but — I've — I've never seen *anything* so funny!"

The father was red in the face, and I thought sure he was going to lose his temper again. "Well, I don't see what's so damned funny about it," he said.

"I'm sorry, Lou," she said, dabbing her eyes with her napkin. She tried to stop, but then a fresh wave of laughter hit her. " 'Is he *here,* Rennie?' 'Is he — *there?*' Old what's-his-name — D'Artagnan — fighting a — a ghost! Zorro! Oh, help! It was so *funny!*"

Now the man was laughing, too. He picked up the knife from beside his plate and made a fake fencing thrust with it toward Rennie. "Take *that*, sir!" he said. "Right through the gizzard! Well, I'll bet I almost got him once or twice. My God, Ren, I must have scared you almost to death."

Rennie had been looking anxiously back and forth at the two of them, but now he seized his knife in one hand and the fork in the other and held them up at full length over his head. "Yowee!" he yelled. "Right through the gizzer! Right through the gizzer!"

They'd gone mad, all three of them. Rennie never even looked at me. He'd forgotten I was there. I got up and left them to their idiot shouting and laughing, and he never saw me go.

It should have ended right there. After that, it was all over with me, and if there were any mercy in this world I should have had done with my master from that moment on. But he wouldn't finish with me. He kept calling me back — not as often as before, but every few days — and, of course, I had to go. I made a brave show of it. I'd appear, my hands in my pockets, nonchalantly whistling, and say "How goes it, Sir Rennie?," but all the time I knew there was no future in it. He didn't demand much of me any more — a few minutes a day. We'd start to plant a vegetable garden (spring was coming on), or swim in a mountain gorge, say, but then Rennie would have enough. He'd turn his back on me, or call to his mother to ask if it was time for them to go out, and I'd be dismissed until the next time.

I think he must have been sorry for me, though. Perhaps that's why he kept me coming back those few times, and perhaps that's why he took me with them on their trip to the country, our last day together.

It was an April Saturday, and the man had got an old car from somewhere to take them all out of the city; maybe it was the car he used in his business. Rennie was in the back seat, and I sat on the edge of the window beside him, watching them all. There had been no demand for my spying talents, of course, and it was the first time I'd seen the other two for weeks.

There didn't seem to be much change in them, except maybe they were quieter. They talked on, the two of them in the front seat, and much of it was still about the same impossible plans: a house in the country, a new job for him, better times. Rennie stayed quiet in the back, sometimes singing to himself, and, outside, the trees streamed by against the sky. We were going to visit friends of theirs in Connecticut.

Rennie went wild when he got there. It wasn't much of a place, as the country goes — a small new house near the top of a sloping field, with four or five other houses in plain sight nearby. There was a scrubby patch of trees near the bottom of the field, and, beyond that, a trickle of marshy brook. But Rennie soaked both his shoes in the water within the first five minutes, and I could see him running about like a small calf just out of the barn, looking at everything, making occasional little leaps straight up in the air, and then pausing to stamp his feet down into a patch of mud. I watched him from the car, where he'd left me.

I thought that was all I was there for, just to keep him company on the dull ride in the car. But shortly before lunch, Rennie called me. He was sitting on a tumble-down stone wall below the house, and the adults were having a cocktail on a porch up above us. The new sun was so warm that we could feel the heat of it in the rocks we sat on. Rennie had scraped his knee somehow, and he was still panting a little from all his running. We didn't talk much — just stayed there and looked at the country. There were touches of pale color showing along the stiff canes of shrubbery beside us, and the new grass in the shallow parts of the brook was already a rich, wet green. There were fat pussy willows everywhere. Somebody had spaded the little garden beside the house, and the smell of fresh clods was in the air. While we sat there, three crows flapped by, not making a sound, and the tops of their wings caught flashes from the sun. Then Rennie's mother called him to come in the house for lunch. He didn't want to go, and just before he left he told me to stay there and keep watching. He ordered me to prepare a report on it for him.

I did as he told me. I worked at it, for I had a sudden hopeful idea that this might lead to something new for us, perhaps a different and less active kind of friendship, but one that would allow me to help him still and so stay near him. I sat there on the wall and took the lay of the land, and then I began to improve it, making it the way my master would like it. I put steeper roofs on the houses round about me, and then I enlarged them and threw up towers and

battlements, all flying silken banners in the sky. I painted
them purple and pink and deep black. Great white horses,
heavy with trappings, clomped out over their drawbridges,
the riders heavily armed against the dangers of the wood.
The woods grew taller and deeper, full of shadows, and the
twisting, rubbery leaves hanging down from their branches
sometimes twitched and rustled with the motions of the wild
animals they concealed. The brook became a torrent, white
and booming, and scarlet birds, trailing long feathery tails,
flew over me. Finally, above it all, I drew a new sky,
brighter and sharper, the color of a yellow crayon.

Rennie didn't come for me after lunch, and I stayed there
on the wall where he'd put me, while the afternoon cooled
and the light began to go. I heard their voices as they went
to the car, and the good-byes, and I thought he'd forgotten
again, in spite of the assignment he'd given me. But then, at
the last instant after they'd closed the car doors, he said,
"Come along, Juck," in a soft voice, and I joined them.

Rennie put me in back, but this time he sat in front, between the other two. I waited there, thinking he would jump
back with me at any moment and ask me for my report. But
we drove along as we were, slowly following all the other
homing cars on the highway, and Rennie was quiet, listening
to the other two talking. It was colder now, and the mother
rolled up the window beside her. I grew desperate, trying to
get my master's attention, trying to give him a sign to remind him I was there, and all the while I kept reviewing
and touching up the lovely surprises I had in store for him.
But then I stopped that, for I knew it would never be
needed.

Rennie did turn around at last, just as we were getting into the outskirts of the city. I could see his face in the shine of the headlights of the car behind us. He gave me a long look over the back of the seat, affectionate and very sleepy. I could feel myself growing dim, disappearing, and I made a last prodigious effort.

"Look, Rennie!" I cried out, like a child to an adult. "Look at me. Watch, now — I'm a dragon! Watch the smoke come out of my mouth!" I know he must have heard me, because for a moment there I could see the slow lashings of my thick scaly tail, but then it was over. He turned away, and I left him for good.

Now I am waiting for my next job, and I don't much care what it will be like. I only hope it will be easy — a quick, simple one, and then an end to it. I wouldn't even mind girls. But I can't choose; I'm not my own master. I have only now learned, after all this time, that this life of mine is hell and that there is no help for it. What hurts me is this new realization that I don't understand their side of it, the grown ones' world. I don't see what's so fine about it — all hard words and broken chairs. I think mine would be a million times better. But Rennie didn't think so. He went over to them, just as they had always known he would, perfectly happily, and, respecting Rennie the way I do, I guess that means there is something there that is better. I see now that the two grownups were never really concerned about me. I wasn't real to them, because all three of them were mixed up with something more important. I was never in it.

Bird of Passage

"THE duty on those French still wines is awfully low, considering," Courtney Allis said, flicking cigarette ash into his empty coffee cup, "so I brought back five cases last summer. Mostly Corton and Clos Vougeot. I picked them up in Beaune. You ought to do the same thing, Pete. It's really the cheapest way to lay down good wines. Just a matter of getting over there, that's all."

"I think I'll do that, Court," said Peter Gillette. "Maybe next summer, if I can get off. Depends what I'm doing."

"Oh, I was going to ask," Allis said. "What *are* you doing these days? Found your new spot yet?"

"No, not yet. I just came back from the Coast, but I don't think that's for me. It'll be something around here, I guess. I'm expecting the word in a few days from one outfit. No use in rushing in, I figure."

Allis shook his head slowly. "Advertising," he said in a wondering tone. "Can't figure it out. Why don't you come on downtown and get in a good, steady business? Nobody suddenly ups and quits a good job down there. You advertising men make too much money, that's what's wrong. Spoils you."

Gillette looked admiringly across the table at his friend, who was finishing the last of his brandy. It was past three o'clock in the afternoon, they were the last pair in the dining room of Allis's club, and still Allis hadn't once spoken of getting back to his desk. Now Gillette looked at his wrist-watch. "Holy smoke!" he said. "Three-thirty-five and I never got to my bank. Now I've got to hunt up some place to cash a check."

"Oh, you can do that here," Allis said easily. "Here, you write it out and I'll get the waiter to take it out to the desk. They charge a dime, though."

"That's O.K.," said Gillette, quickly taking out a check-book. He looked across the table at Allis. "Hundred too much?"

"As long as it doesn't ricochet, Pete," Allis said, smiling. "A small kite we'll permit, but no bouncing. Big weekend coming up?"

"Could be, Court, could be." Frowning slightly, Gillette filled out the check. It was too late now, of course, but he realized that he could perfectly well have said two hundred.

Feeling the pleasant warmth of the brandy in his stomach, Gillette walked slowly down Madison Avenue in the cold afternoon sunlight. He might just as well, he thought, stop in at his liquor store and order a few bottles of wine. Nothing wrong in that. He could ask them to set the stuff aside for a couple of weeks and he would pay when he picked it up. By that time he might have a place where he could put the wine. Now that he had a destination, he walked more briskly, admiring the pretty, expensively dressed young women who came toward him, furs swinging, heels clicking, their intent young faces bright in the chilly air. As always, he felt the excitement of being part of the great New York crowd, with its purposeful speed, its sure sense of destinations, its shining air of promise and accomplishment. He stopped to look at some bolts of cloth in a shirtmaker's window, and then again to study a display of antique jewelry. Looking in the window, he could see himself palely reflected against the moving traffic, his face tan and well shaved above his neat chesterfield, his figured silk tie, and his expensive new shoes. As he stood there he felt a hand on his arm and a man beside him said, "Hey, Pete!"

Startled, he spun around and took a backward step. "Oh," he said. "It's you, Howard." He took his hand out of his coat pocket and then quickly put it back in again. "I haven't seen you for a long time."

"Not for a hell of a long time," Howard Shea said, slapping him on the shoulder. "Months anyway. Why'n't you drop around once in a while? The office doesn't seem the same without you. People might think you didn't like the old place or something."

"I've been away," Gillette said. "Out in California."

"Well, you haven't missed much," Shea said cheerfully. "R. and S. carries on. Josie Carpenter had a baby. Old man Krueger down in Media had a heart attack and had to quit for six months. Gunner Swift even went on the wagon, no kidding this time. You see — just dull. We missed you during the football pools last fall. Nobody even knew where you'd gone, the way you up and quit so fast. I even asked Phil Sabin —"

"Oh, how is Phil these days?"

"Fine, fine. I even asked him where you were but he said he didn't know. I thought he might have had a letter or something."

"No. You know how it is when you're traveling. Well . . ." Gillette held his hand out this time. "I have to run, Howard. Damned good to see you again." He shook hands and started down the avenue. Then he turned around and hurried after Shea. "Oh, Howard," he said quickly. "Almost forgot. Look, old man, don't say anything to Phil Sabin about running into me like this, will you? You see, I — I want to drop in and surprise him next week. He doesn't even know I'm around here and I thought I'd come in and say hello. Give him a surprise. He'd get a big bang out of it. Just don't tell anybody, huh? You see."

"Why, sure thing, Pete," Shea said. He looked at Gillette curiously. "I won't breathe a word. And I'll see you next week then."

"What? Oh, sure, sure. See you then, Howard, and thanks."

When Gillette reached the end of the block, he turned and found the back of Shea's overcoat receding in the crowds. Little sneak, he thought. Prying little man. Almost surely, he decided, Shea knew nothing about it — he wasn't that good an actor. That meant that Phil Sabin hadn't told the R. & S. staff what had happened — at least not all of them. But why was Shea so curious about his leaving R. & S.?

A man could quit his job, couldn't he? He didn't have to go around telling every hundred-dollar copy writer his reasons. Gillette remembered that he had always disliked Shea, with his bonhomie and his perpetual smile. He hated his petty little show of family pride in the baby pictures on his desk, hated the precise way he departed on the dot of five-thirty for his home in Queens. Run home, little white mouse. Stick close to the wall. Gillette remembered that once, as Phil Sabin's executive assistant, he had been going over expense accounts and had caught Shea putting in for six dollars' worth of phantom taxi fares. Shea had been terrified when he had warned him about it. Little man! Gillette suddenly realized that he was trembling. He forgot about his wines, and turned and almost ran back to his hotel.

A thin man with rimless spectacles passed Gillette as he walked down his hotel corridor. Gillette went right past the door to his room and then stopped and lit a cigarette. He turned slowly and saw that the man was getting into the elevator. Gillette took out his key, and for a moment he held his breath as he stood in front of the door to his room and listened. There was no sound. Quickly he opened the door, shut it behind him, and glanced about the room. Nobody. He dropped the cigarette in an ashtray, threw his hat and coat on the bed, and knelt beside his two closed suitcases. They were still locked, the way he had left them. Nobody had been in the room, nobody had been snooping. He straightened up, feeling suddenly tired, and then started and almost cried out at the shattering sound of the telephone bell. He stared at the phone as it rang three or four times on the bedside table, and then with a quick movement he strode over and took the receiver off the hook. "What is it?" he asked in a flat, impersonal voice.

"Hello, Peter?" his brother said. "That you, Peter?"

Hating himself for his fears, Gillette sat down on the bed. "It's me, Martin," he said. He sounded bored. "Still tailing me? Still being Head of the Family?"

"Listen, Pete," his brother said, "I've been trying to get you all day. I've been calling all over. Now, listen to me."

"Say," Gillette said in a suspicious tone. "How'd you know where I was?"

"A guess. A smart guess. I knew you'd pick nothing but the best."

"O.K., wise guy," Gillette said, his voice getting high and angry. "Now you can listen to *me*. I'm not coming back, see? You can just save your breath. I'm through with sitting around that creepy apartment of yours. I'm through borrowing five bucks from you for a haircut. I've had it, see? And you can tell Eunice I'm through watching that superior look on her face, and I'm through ducking out of the room while she lies to her society girl friends about poor Brother Pete having a nervous breakdown. And the same thing goes for that phony Dr. Marston, too. Tell him for me I don't need any psychiatrist to hold my hand. I feel fine, see? Oh, and one more thing. Tell your little helpmeet I'm through having her snooping through my mail, too."

"She never — Oh, what the hell," Martin said in a tired voice. "Are you finished? O.K., then. First, we don't want you back. As a matter of fact, I'm not calling from home, I came out to this phone booth. I don't suppose they'd tap my phone, but I'm not taking any chances. You see, they've been here, the District Attorney's office. At last count they have eleven bum checks, including the one you gave that Mr. and Mrs. Fowler in Dallas for fifteen hundred. I thought *they* were friends of yours."

"You sound pretty smug about it all, you son of a bitch," Gillette said. His hand holding the telephone was shaking. "I suppose Phil Sabin put you up to this."

"Phil Sabin did call me, Pete. He wanted to know if I wanted to make the checks good. You see, they've all come back to him, since you still seem to be passing yourself off as an R. and S. executive. And why are you so sore at him, anyway? He kept you out of jail, didn't he? He let us try to pay the company back. Well, anyway, I told him no. I said we were through putting it up for you. My savings are down the drain and Eunice has gone into hers, too, much as you hate her for it. And all for nothing, as far as I can see." Martin was shouting now. "All for nothing, Peter! All for nothing! Eighteen thousand bucks so far and still not half of it. You try scraping up eighteen thousand bucks in cash sometime — Oh, I *beg* your pardon. You already have."

There was a little silence, and then Martin started speaking again, in a quieter voice. "I'm sorry. That doesn't help. Listen, I just called for one thing. Give it up, Pete. Come on in. They're sure to get you now, and it'll be easier for everyone if you just give up. I'm not going to tell them where you are, but I wish you'd do that. You're just on the edge of being caught every minute now. I should think you'd feel better once it was over, no matter what."

"Martin," Gillette said in a shaking voice, "do one thing for me first. Tell me where Peggy is."

"That's the one thing I can't do, Pete. Peggy's gone away for a while. I know where she is but I can't tell you. You see, she's afraid of you."

"Why, you —" Gillette slammed the receiver down. Afraid, he thought. Peggy afraid of *me?* After all we've been. Why, we'd have been married by now if it hadn't been for this thing. All those plans, and then the little coward turns and runs the moment she hears about it. That's women for you — demanding, expecting things of you, frighteningly strong one minute and then cold and gone away the next. Bitches, bitches all! You can't count on one of them. But Peggy — she never really heard my side of it. Maybe now? Maybe Martin's just lying about her. Maybe she's been trying to find me all this time. He grabbed the telephone and asked for her number. As he sat on the bed and listened to the distant bell ring and ring, a drop of sweat rolled off his forehead and onto his hand and suddenly he felt the tightness in his throat and the shaking in his chest. Oh God, he thought, not again. But the tears came, and he replaced the telephone and sat there crying helplessly, choking on the familiar, heavy lump of terror in his chest.

About a minute later he scrambled to his feet and wiped his face with both hands. Reaching into his pants pocket, he took out a bunch of keys and quickly unlocked the bigger of the two suitcases. He felt under his shirts and found, beside the little stack of checkbooks tied with a rubber band, the bulky parcel made by the wrapped gun. Hastily he unwound the undershirt that bound it and took out the heavy, oily Army-issue .45 automatic. It was quite dark in the unlighted room by now, and he carried the gun over by the window, where he unlatched the safety. The slide made a loud click as it snapped back into place, and Gillette, trying to hold his arm steady, raised the big pistol and pointed it slowly about the room, first at the vague outlines of the bathroom door and then at the gleam of light on the glass doorknob of the closet. Then, keeping his finger away from the trigger, he aimed the gun at his head, first pointing it at his temple and then gently touching the muzzle to his ear. When he felt the cold metal against his skin, his whole body jerked spasmodically and the gun slid out of his sweaty hand and crashed to the floor. He kicked the ugly thing violently across the room and stood trembling by the dark window, feeling the tears and the sweat run down his face and onto his shirt. A few moments later he picked up the phone and ordered a highball.

By the time the bellhop rapped on Gillette's door with the drink, he had taken off his shirt, washed his face in cold water, and was tying the cord of his red silk bathrobe. He wrote his name and room number on the back of the bill, handed the boy a dollar, and said, "Tell the room clerk I'll be checking out in an hour or so, son. Just got a call I have to get back to the Coast."

When the boy went out, Gillette drained half the highball, lit a cigarette, and carried the glass and the cigarette into the bathroom. Although he had shaved that morning, he carefully put a new blade into his razor and, humming lightly, began to lather his face. Much better, he thought. Much, much better.

Gillette smiled at his mental picture of Phil Sabin's face when the checks had started to come in, but then he stopped humming as he found himself thinking again of that morning, five months before, when Sabin had called him into his office and asked him to shut the door. "No you won't," Sabin had said quietly at one point, the phony vouchers in his hand. "You won't shoot yourself, because you haven't got the guts. At least I don't think you will, and anyway I guess I don't give a damn." And then, like a fool, Gillette had pleaded with him, had begged like the cheapest little stenographer begging for her job.

A man like that, Gillette thought, scraping carefully around his chin, can afford not to understand a mistake. A man like that can afford to be moral at fifty thousand a year. Phil Sabin, my pal. Phil Sabin, my drinking buddy with a weakness for Stingers. My golfing partner with a weakness for big bets. My boss with a weakness for letting me do the dirty work. Probably he was watching me all the time. What about those six handmade, monogrammed shirts I gave him for Christmas? How'd he think I could do that sort of thing on two-fifty a week? He was laying for me, that's what. Letting me get in good and deep. And now this bit about not telling the office what happened to me. Probably he's patting himself on the back, telling himself that's the noble thing. Giving me my chance, the little hypocrite. Oh, a real Christer, Phil Sabin! He knows damn well that'll really get the rumors and cheap talk going around about me, even with jerks like Howard Shea.

All *right*, then! They've had their chance — Sabin and Peggy and Brother Martin and all of them. Now they can sweat for me. Let *them* do the worrying now. Oh, I'll give them a chase, all right! All I ask — he leaned forward and stared at his face in the steamy mirror, shaking the razor gently at himself — all I ask is one chance at Phil Sabin. Oh, nothing rough, of course. Nothing stupid and violent. Perhaps one of those dogs of his, one of those ugly Boxers he's so nuts about. There must be some simple way, something perfectly painless you can give them. I'll just think about that.

Gillette dressed quickly but carefully, taking time to pick out the right necktie and tuck a fresh handkerchief into his breast pocket. Conscious of the smell of his shaving lotion, conscious of the calmness and speed of his mind, he found the gun under his bed, wrapped it up, took out a new checkbook, and repacked and locked his suitcase. When he looked at his watch, it was five forty-two. Five forty-two on Friday night — R. & S. closed, the banks closed, everything closed until Monday. Grinning suddenly, he took out his wallet and extracted from it his company air-travel card. "Very careless," he said aloud. "Very careless, Phil, old boy. This trip is on you." Thinking of his own cleverness in not using the card until now, he again wished he could see Phil Sabin's face, this time when the bill for this trip came in. He almost giggled as he looked up the telephone number of the airline. "This is Mr. Gillette, of Roebling and Sabin," he said into the telephone. "Peter Gillette, executive manager. Can you squeeze me onto a Miami plane this evening? It's very important and Mr. Sabin would appreciate it if . . . Oh, you can? . . . Fine. Fine. Seven o'clock from the terminal. . . . I'll pick it up myself before then. Thank you. We'll remember this."

Down in the hotel lobby, Gillette had only to look at the stupid, polite face of the man behind the marble counter to know he was all right. It was taking no chance, no chance at all. "Peter Gillette," he said, thrusting an engraved R. & S. card across at him. "West Coast manager. A check all right? It's a New York bank. I need a little cash, too. Say seventy-five? You can telephone the office if you —"

"That's perfectly all right, Mr. Gillette."

Slowly, savoring the taste of excitement in his mouth, Gillette wrote out the check. When the bills came, he tapped them into a neat pile and thrust them into his wallet, buttoned his overcoat, and lit a cigarette. As he inhaled, he saw that the man behind the counter was watching him. Curious? Suspicious? No, the man was simply envious, admiring. Gillette stared back at him coolly until the man dropped his eyes and pretended to look at a pile of letters on the counter. Of course. They were all afraid of him, really. Martin was afraid. Only Peggy had come right out and said so. The world was always afraid of a man of imagination, always had been. Oh, they would try to make him play their game, try to make *him* afraid. And they would try to bring him down — like ants pulling down a tiger. And perhaps, looking at it honestly, they might catch him someday, with their puny plots, their tricky telephone calls, their little worried conferences, their laws. But he was through with fear now, he knew that. He would pay them back, every one of them. And he would not be stopped. He was on his way at last.

Holding the cigarette between his lips, he carefully pulled on his pigskin gloves and turned to follow the bellboy with his bags across the thick carpets. In the window of the lobby florist shop he could see the reflection of his neat tie, the glint of his shiny, expensive shoes as he strode out toward the door and the waiting taxi.

In an Early Winter

IT was a narrow, two-lane highway, and on this sunny
Saturday afternoon the traffic heading away from the
city was heavy. Five cars in front of the Scullins, a diesel
trailer truck labored up the hill, changed gears, and went on
with a louder, shriller roar. Scullin watched while two cars
swept down the hill and past them, then pulled his convertible out into the left-hand lane and gunned it. Slowly at
first, and then with sudden speed, they gained on the line of
cars. Scullin kept his foot clamped down on the accelerator
until they were within a hundred feet of the crest of the
hill, braked sharply, and angled into the narrow space between the back of the truck and the following automobile.
Amanda Scullin uncurled her toes and murmured, "Whew!"

"Stupid ants!" her husband said. "All these weekend
jockeys know is Follow the Leader. You weren't scared
were you, Mandy?"

"Oh, no," Amanda said lightly. "I just pushed a hole in
the floorboards, that's all."

"Well, don't be. I know what I'm doing. I'm really a very
good driver." The road on the other side of the hill was

empty, and they passed the truck and raced smoothly along between rough-heaped stone walls and a double row of maple trees, bare and shining in the winter sunlight. It was a cold and crystal day, the end of a whole week of early-winter frost, and there were bright patches of frozen snow scattered about the bumpy fields and piled in the lee of big, gray-shingled barns. But it was warm inside the car, and the hum of the heater and the rush of the wind past the windows made a steady, comfortable roar. Amanda lit a cigarette and leaned back next to her husband, rubbing her ear against the roughness of his overcoat. It was, she decided, a perfect day, a day to remember. And Joe, almost surely, *was* a fine driver. He simply drove a car the way he did everything else — with dash, with an aura of adventure and physical pleasure, with an abrupt youthfulness that matched his undergraduate flannels, his graying but crew-cut hair, and the way he sometimes upset ashtrays with his hands when he was talking vehemently. And this careless intensity was what, so far in their brief life together, she loved most about her husband.

They had been married for exactly three weeks. They had known each other a little more than two months, and it was their favorite joke that Joe had literally thrown himself at her head. Amanda — who had been Amanda Ballantine, thirty-two years old, unmarried, and (she had finally decided) not pretty but interesting-looking — had taken her vacation in the fall, leaving behind her job as a buyer of handbags and accessories for a New York department store, and flying to Jamaica. It was her first visit to the Caribbean and her first vacation alone, and she had quickly been forced to admit that it was a shocking mistake. After five days, she was bored with shopping in smelly back alleys for big straw hats and bottles of thick rum; tired of seeing the languid sights from the sun-smitten back seat of a jolting carriage; disgusted with the prospect of drinking more planters' punches with the two skinny British divorcees who shared the hotel room across the hall from hers, and who whispered to her the precise details of their ex-husbands' infidelities and eccentricities; and fed up with swimming alone, seeing two-year-old movies, writing lying messages on the back of impossibly colored postcards, and dancing stiffly and silently with the assistant manager of the hotel. In this mood, she had been sitting beside the hotel tennis court one afternoon, sullenly watching a violent game of men's doubles, when one of the players, chasing a cross-court shot, dashed suddenly toward her, stumbled, and rocketed her off her lawn chair. That had been her meeting with Joe Scullin. Although she was not hurt, he had been truly appalled. "Good God!" he kept repeating. "I might have broken your neck!" He had insisted on giving up his game and taking her inside for a drink.

Amanda still found it hard to put much credence in what happened after that. She was a careful girl, the only daughter of two careful parents, who had married late and had their child late. Her father, up to the time of his death, had played exactly nine holes of golf every Saturday from May 15th to October 15th; had worn a sweater under his suit coat to the office; had drunk one highball before dinner on Friday and Saturday nights. Her mother, who now lived in Tucson, had tended a small, neat suburban flower garden and a small, neat suburban house, filled with Currier & Ives prints and furniture covered in flowered chintz. She replaced the slipcovers every second March. Amanda had grown up with the sure knowledge of how life should be lived, and to this day she read with a good, strong light over her right shoulder, went to bed on the first day of a head cold, never ate pork that was faintly pink, and didn't go swimming until two hours after lunch. She shook hands firmly, plucked her eyebrows lightly but never used mascara, and believed that happiness lay in self-knowledge. She had reminded herself constantly of this, her true, unexcitable nature, during the week when Joe Scullin accompanied her everywhere in Jamaica, taking her shopping and sight-seeing and dancing and swimming, drinking planters' punches with her, leading her to a midnight cockfight in the back room of a grocery store, teaching her to stand up at the net and volley back hard ground strokes without flinching. Amanda was aware of the improbable, violent manner of their meeting, suspicious of the smell of jasmine and bougainvillaea and the warmth of the nights, cautiously bewaring of Joe's six feet two and his history. (He was a widower, a former college pole vaulter, a New York importer.) All through that week, she pictured herself as a stock figure, an old maid in the tropics. And although Joe was thirty-five, she thought of herself somehow as being the older of the two — the responsible, slower-moving elder with a thought for the morrow.

Nevertheless, two days before the end of her vacation, she had cabled her office and changed her tickets, booking passage to New York on the boat with Joe. She had been prepared for this movie to end at the pier in New York, but it hadn't ended. They had been married in her apartment on the day before Christmas, and had served the Jamaica rum to a small party made up of Joe's parents, Joe's college roommate, and three girls from her office. Even then, Amanda had been so aware of the headlong, shockingly non-typical thing she had done that she hadn't dared write to her mother about it until four days after the wedding.

Now, on their way to visit Joe's parents, who lived forty miles up the Hudson from New York, Amanda yawned in the warm car. They had been working hard all morning, arranging and discarding their books, and she was pleasantly weary. "How much farther is it?" she asked.

"Pretty soon," Joe said, patting her knee. "We turn off this road in another mile or so."

"I may go to sleep," she said, tucking her legs up on the seat. She closed her eyes. "I *never* used to go to sleep in the daytime," she said happily. "You're making me over. You're going to make me fat and lazy."

"Good. That's the way to be — relaxed."

"Like you?"

"Sure, like me. Look at you — you can't even fall asleep without feeling guilty about it." Confidently, he recited what Amanda already recognized as his maxims: "Take it easy. Have fun. Do what you want to do."

"I am," Amanda said. "Tell me about your family's house. What's it like?"

"Well, it's a big old place. Clapboards. It's near the river. It's — well, I guess you could call it relaxed, too. Nothing fancy." He peered forward and said, "Here's the turnoff. Only five miles more from here."

Scullin slowed the car for the turn, but not enough. When they swung onto the narrow side road, the wheels caught a small patch of ice, and the car slewed sickeningly, almost at right angles to the road. They rushed for the ditch as Joe yanked on the wheel. Then the tires bounced sharply off something on the side of the road and the car straightened out again.

"Look *out*, Joe!" Amanda shouted, grabbing his arm.

"Sorry," her husband said, picking up speed again. "Little slick place back there. They never plow decently around here. No damage done."

Amanda said nothing, but she was no longer sleepy. For the rest of the trip, she sat stiffly upright, nervously watching the road and the trees that rushed toward them out of the gathering dusk.

Amanda had never seen a place quite like the Scullins'. A big, heavy-browed porch ran completely around the house, with heavy vines twisted about its railings. A canoe paddle, a faded croquet ball, and three splayed wicker chairs were scattered near the front door. Inside, there was a narrow, dark hall leading back to the stairs, and off it, to the right, a huge living room ran the full length of the building. There was a big fireplace at the far end. The bricks, and even the woodwork above the fireplace, were smudged with soot, and the mantelpiece held two tarnished silver teapots, pewter candelabra without candles, and a careless stack of letters.

Part of the bookcase across from the windows evidently served as a bar, for there were bottles and cocktail shakers and corkscrews ranged in it, along with a great heap of used corks lying in an earthenware bowl. There were no rugs on the floor, which was made of handsome, much-scuffed wide planks. A scratched, high phonograph stood away from the wall in one corner, its lid open, and there were dusty stacks of records on the floor beside it. The house smelled vaguely of cooking food and fresh paint. But the heavy red curtains were drawn, there was a fire in the fireplace, and Amanda, who was accustomed to smaller, newer, more careful rooms, was almost immediately excited and charmed by the place. They found Mrs. Scullin reclining on a huge, bent old sofa, holding an Old-Fashioned and reading a magazine. There was a cane propped beside her, and on her right foot she was wearing a green felt slipper.

"Can't get up!" she cried cheerfully. "Come and kiss me, Amanda."

"Good Lord," Joe said, putting down their suitcases. "Not again! What was it this time?"

"Oh, it's nothing, Joey. Really nothing at all. You see, a fuse blew out and I broke my toe."

Joe began to laugh. "I don't get it," he said. "But trust you to find some way to do it differently."

"I know, I know. Make yourselves a drink — you must be *frozen*. Lewis is out in the garage, cleaning paintbrushes or something. He started to paint the hall bookcase this morning, believe it or not. But then, of course, he thought of something else, and spent all afternoon trying to fix the car, so I guess it'll have to go to the garage again. And one of its front doors is always coming open. No, Joey, you *know* how the fuses here are always going out. These old circuits just aren't made for conveniences. Well, there I was in the kitchen the other night, peacefully ironing, when — snap! — utter darkness. Well, I started for somewhere — I wasn't just going to *stand* there in my tomb — when I bumped into the silly ironing board and the iron came down on my toe. But it's all right. Dr. Parmalee says a couple of weeks hobbling around on this cane and I'll be fine. Amanda, you really look *incredibly* lovely!"

Amanda blushed and took a glass from her husband. Joe stood beside her, smiling across at his mother. "Last year, she broke her wrist by stepping on the dog," he said admiringly.

"Well, he *would* lie there in the dark at the foot of the stairs, poor thing," said Mrs. Scullin. "Joey, take Amanda upstairs to your room and then go find your father." She heaved herself upright and picked up her cane. "I'm going to creak out to the kitchen and poke at our dinner, and Amanda can come down and talk to me when she's ready. If you want, dear, of course."

"Oh, can't I do it, please?" Amanda said. "You shouldn't be up."

"Nonsense," Mrs. Scullin said, finishing her Old-Fashioned. "Joey, make me another of these, dear, will you? No, Amanda, I just want to gossip with you. I want us to be terribly good friends."

In the kitchen, Mrs. Scullin moved a heap of old newspapers off a stool and made Amanda sit there while she cooked the dinner. Amanda drank her whiskey and watched her mother-in-law with a rather stunned sense of pleasure and discovery. Her own mother had always had maids and had always looked overdressed and uneasy in her spotless kitchen. Mrs. Scullin was wearing faded tan slacks, a soft leather jerkin, and heavy silver bracelets. Somehow, in spite of her almost white hair, the costume was charming. She stood in front of the old oilstove, propping herself on her cane with one hand and stirring a sauce with the other, a cigarette between her lips and her eyes squinted against the smoke. An ash fell on the stove and she brushed it away. "Tell me, Amanda," she said. "Are you *passionately* happy?"

Amanda blushed again, feeling like an awkward girl of thirteen. She wasn't accustomed to searching, personal questions. "Why, I guess so," she said at last. "I guess I'm still not used to it all. But I *am* happy."

"Because I want you to be," Mrs. Scullin went on. "I have an idea you're a very *nice* girl, much too nice for Joey. And I do hope you're going to like us and this rackety old house. We're an awfully Tobacco Road bunch, as you can see. But we get along and have fun. This place needs you, Amanda, and I hope you'll come out here *always*. I'm much too lazy and silly to plan things properly and get things done. But you strike me as a collected woman — a proper housewife, who gets all the vegetables cooked on time and then can talk affairs of *state* with the man on her right at dinner, looking perfectly ravishing in a black Dior. Now, where's that damned marjoram got to? I hope Lewis remembered to open the wine."

Warmed by her drink and the heat of the stove, lulled by the flow of Mrs. Scullin's affectionate, featherheaded conversation, Amanda perched on her stool and tasted an old and gentle excitement, the expectation of a young child who has been allowed in the kitchen to watch the preparations for a party. She could hear the thump of feet and the sound of male voices and laughter from the next room. There was a bunch of chrysanthemums in a copper vase over the stove, and the smell of the rich sauce cooking made Amanda ravenous. She felt safe and at home with her new family.

After dinner, Amanda sat on the big sofa, and the Scullins' old Labrador retriever came and curled up at her feet. Mrs. Scullin played delicate little Handelian tunes on a battered recorder while Mr. Scullin and Joe sat on the floor in front of the fire and cleaned a shotgun. The two men, Amanda decided, looked very much alike as they talked, their long legs extended in front of them. Mr. Scullin was thinner and even taller than Joe, his short hair was completely white, and he had a long, thin scar that angled across his forehead and into one eyebrow. Half alseep from the wine and the music, Amanda lay back and scratched the dog with her toe, listening to Joe and his father, and their exchange of old stories — names and reminiscences that were strange to her now but would in time become warm household familiarities. Finally, Mrs. Scullin put down the recorder and pointed toward the disassembled gun on the floor. "It's a good thing you weren't here this morning, Amanda," she said. "Honestly, the *gunnery* around here! It sounded like Waterloo. And the complaints!"

"Oh, hell," said Mr. Scullin, smiling at her. "Just two shots. And little neighbor Snavely again. Snavely the sniveller."

"It was the starlings again, Joey," Mrs. Scullin went on. "A perfect *cloud* of them came into the pear tree at lunchtime. So Lewis leaped up from the table, grabbed the gun and ran out, and — boom! Then there was this cry of absolute *horror* from down the hill, and Snavely came running up with his face all red and said he'd have to call the police again. I thought at least Lewis had slain one of his awful schnauzers."

"Did you hit his house, or something?" Joe asked.

"Of course not," Mr. Scullin said, still smiling. "He's just the nervous type, that's all. Perfectly safe."

"Well, you did shower his porch once, Lewis," said Mrs. Scullin. "I'm not at all sure I can blame the poor man."

"That was just some shot pellets that fell there, that once," Mr. Scullin said. "The day Joey and I were shooting up the Guy Lombardo records." He assembled the gun, snapped the last part into place, and aimed the weapon about the room. "I'll bet Snavely's never even held a shotgun. That's what's wrong with him. People like that are always jumpy." He winked at his wife, and then said, "Joey, did you ever tell your wife about *your* hunting accident?"

"My accident? *My accident?*" Joe said in a tone of mock outrage. Apparently it was an old family joke. "I wasn't even *there!*"

"Well, you'd better tell Amanda, dear," Mrs. Scullin said comfortably. "You've probably got her terrified."

"It was in college," Joe said to his wife, with evident relish. "I had this .22 in my room, and a man visiting my roommate picked it up. Well, it was loaded and the thing went off and scared him and Walt just about to death. I'd had it on safety, but he must have flipped it off. Nobody was hurt, of course, but the funny part of it was that the slug went into the closet and perforated six suits of Walt's hanging there. It cost him forty bucks' worth at the invisible menders. My God, he was mad!"

"Goodness!" said Amanda. Then she noticed that all the Scullins were watching her with something like pride in their faces, and she was aware that she had perhaps sounded rather shocked. She forced a little laugh. "Things certainly *happen* in this family, don't they?"

"They certainly do, my dear," said Mrs. Scullin, groping for her cane. "You'll just have to get used to it. After all, Joey had to knock you down to meet you. But remind me someday to tell you how Lewis almost drowned me on our honeymoon. That damned canoe!" She got to her feet. "Children, I'm going to bed. Lewis, try to remember this time to pour some water on the fire before you come up. I don't want to find the place in ashes in the morning. Good night, all."

But it was Amanda who remembered to extinguish the fire, a few minutes later, after she and the two men had started upstairs. She came back, filled a teakettle in the kitchen, and emptied it on the coals. Standing in the dark living room, she watched the clouds of steam and ashes fly up, and listened to the loud, cheerful voices of the family upstairs. There was something about the evening just past — some vague recurring dissonance — that flickered on the edges of her memory. But in her weariness she could not bring it into focus. She looked carefully around the room but could find no fire screen. Upstairs, she drew a bath and lay back in the tub, trying to recapture her earlier mood of sleepy euphoria. She found herself staring up at the bathroom light. It was an old-fashioned fixture, a single naked bulb that hung down from the ceiling on rusty metal links. Lying in the tub, it suddenly occurred to her that she was almost directly under the bulb; the shiny brass chain that turned the light on and off seemed to be dangling just above her forehead. Suppose that old ceiling plaster, wet with so many years of steam . . . Or suppose somebody stood up in the tub and reached out . . . Amanda sat up and quickly finished her bath. Drying herself with a big, soft towel, she was angry at herself for her old maid's fears. She was not being controlled, she told herself firmly. The light, she could see now, was not really directly over the tub.

Lying in bed, Amanda felt nervous and wakeful, and she snuggled next to her husband. And then, just as she was finally falling off to sleep, she felt Joe stir beside her. Instantly, she was wide awake, alarm bells ringing inside her. "Joe!" she said sharply. "Joe! You're not smoking, are you?"

"What?" he said indistinctly. "Smoking? No, I'm sleeping. What's the matter with you, anyway? Go to sleep."

When Amanda awoke the next morning, Joe had already dressed and gone downstairs. For a few minutes, she lay in bed, sleepily listening to the sound of footsteps from the living room below, hoping that her husband would come up and close the window and talk to her. Finally, she got up and closed it herself. Lifting the shade, she peered out at three cold locust trees and the scraggly, frost-heaved lawn that slanted unevenly away from the house. It was a gray, lowering day; the sky above the trees was full of hurrying shapes and omens, and Amanda could see, above the slate roof of the next house down the hill, the dull sheen of ice on the river. She shivered in the cold and hurried back to the warm bed. When she awoke again, it was to the coughing and rattling of an engine and the shrill cry of a power saw, coming from somewhere behind the house. She looked at her watch and found that it was almost noon. She arose and dressed hastily and went downstairs, looking for a cup of coffee. In the dark hall at the foot of the stairs, she almost stumbled over a can of paintbrushes, which stood beside the freshly painted wooden bookcase.

A few minutes later, carrying her second cup of coffee and smoking a cigarette, she looked into the empty living room and then found her mother-in-law sitting in the little book-lined study across the hall. Mrs. Scullin, her injured foot up on a cracked-leather ottoman, was painting her fingernails. Today, she was wearing slim corduroy slacks of a pale green.

"Come in, my dear," she said, cheerfully waving her stiff, outspread fingers. "I'm just trying a divine new ten-cent-store shade. Really for teen-agers. How nice you had such a lovely long sleep." With her other hand, she cleared the scattered heap of Sunday newspapers that lay beside her on the couch. "Come and sit here beside me and do your nails, too. It'll look so much more becoming on you. I'm afraid the boys woke you up with their awful saw. Such energy for Sunday! Just the way they used to be together when Joey came back from school on his vacations. They've already finished that painting on the old hall bookcase, and now they're cutting firewood or something behind the garage. I'm afraid they spattered paint all over the hall floor. Just like them! They're so *alike*, don't you feel?"

Feeling indolent and feminine, Amanda sat in the study for an hour with Mrs. Scullin while they painted their nails and read the newspapers and gossiped about clothes and concerts and Joe's favorite dishes and Amanda's job and her childhood. Mrs. Scullin looked through the shelves and found an album of family photographs, and showed Amanda pictures of Joe as a small boy — on horseback in Montana, holding a dead snake at summer camp — an older Joe in a canoe with an Airedale on a small lake, all the Scullins and three strangers eating sandwiches on some mountaintop, Joe (in his college-letter sweater) at the tiller of a catboat at Cape Cod.

Mrs. Scullin had rambling, surprising anecdotes to tell about almost all the pictures ("That was the summer we all went out West in that awful old Essex, and I caught some strange bug and was sick in a hotel room in Missoula for ten days." . . . "This was the year when Lewis was so broke and we couldn't pay Joey's summer-camp bill until the next spring. Or maybe it was the year before"), and Amanda, who had always spent her summers at the same proper seaside resort in New Jersey, tried hard to remember all the adventures and keep track of all the places where the Scullins had stayed. Finally, on the last pages of the book, there were pictures of Joe's first wife, Rosemary. Amanda looked gravely at her predecessor — a tall, long-legged girl with shoulder-length black hair and a wide mouth — and tried to find a meaning in the tiny pictures, some link between this dead woman, this pretty, lost stranger, and herself.

Mrs. Scullin took the book from her and replaced it on the shelf. "You have no idea what a difference you've made in Joey," she said quickly, sounding ill at ease at last. "Since he's married you, he's his old self. You've made him *terribly* happy. Nothing like the way he's been this last year and a half since — since she died."

"It must have been awful," Amanda said slowly. Her husband had barely talked to her about Rosemary, and she was curious and at the same time afraid to hear about her. "It was heart, wasn't it? Was she sick for a long time?"

"Heavens, no!" cried Mrs. Scullin. "My dear, hasn't Joey *told* you? Well, I'm not sure I should be the one. But then you've got to know about it sometime, I guess." Mrs. Scullin paused, looking distracted, and lit a cigarette. Amanda waited, her eyes on the floor.

"Well, it was in Maine," Mrs. Scullin finally went on, speaking quickly. "And it was *very* sudden. That was what was so awful. Why, we'd all *known* Rosemary had something funny about her heart. Some little thing. Goodness, we all used to talk about it and — you know, even joke about it. But we never dreamed it was anything, really. Not even Joey. Well, that summer the two of them went to Maine for Joey's vacation. Somewhere up near Camden . . ."

Amanda listened carefully, like someone following a story that was being read aloud from a book, as she attempted, without hope, to imagine her husband on a vacation with a strange wife, in a place she had never seen.

". . . and they ended up that afternoon taking a long

swim. Rosemary was a wonderful swimmer, almost as good as Joey. She was always like that. Joey has always liked doing strenuous, exciting things, and Rosemary could do them, too, right along with him. But this time, when she came out, she'd hurt herself somehow. She'd got too cold, or too tired, or something. Anyway, she told Joey she wasn't feeling too well, and when they got back to the cottage, she thought she'd just lie down before dinner. And then, when he went up to wake her, he found her . . . He found out."

Amanda turned her head to hide the tears in her eyes. "Was the doctor there by then?" she asked, after a moment. "Did he call the doctor when she felt sick? Because of her heart?"

"Why, no," Mrs. Scullin said vaguely. "At least, I don't think so. Because, just as I said, we'd never *imagined* it was anything." And then she went on, talking faster and faster, sounding — it seemed to Amanda — suddenly anxious to get the account over with. "But when the doctor did come, later, he told Joey *not* to blame himself. He said it again and again. He said you could almost call it a medical accident." She paused and then burst out again, like a child faced with a difficult problem in homework. "Oh, Amanda!" she cried. "I don't *understand* these things! I'm not a doctor!"

Her voice trailed off, and the two women sat in silence in the little room. "It was an *accident*, Amanda," Mrs. Scullin said again. "It was nobody's fault."

Amanda blew her nose, and bent down and picked up the bottles of nail polish and polish remover from the floor. Then the front door banged open and the two men came into the hall, stamping their feet and bringing a great rush of cold air in with them.

"Hi, you two!" Joe said loudly, coming into the study. He kissed Amanda. "Hi, you slugabed. We just cut up almost a cord of wood while you were pounding your ear. We did most of two whole trees that went down in the last hurricane. And before *that* we painted!" Both he and his father had streaming eyes, bright-red cheeks and noses and ears, and tousled hair. In their striped scarves and ragged country sweaters, they looked like two schoolboys. Now Joe held out two pairs of old hockey skates to her in his mittened hands. "Look what I found in the garage! They're not very sharp, but Mother's old pair will fit you with a couple of extra pairs of socks. We can go out after lunch. It's a wonderful day for skating."

"Oh, but I'm such a dreadful skater," said Amanda. "My ankles are like Jello. And it's so cold."

"Nonsense," Joe said. "It's just right if you keep moving. And the river is frozen for almost a half mile out. *That* hasn't happened for years around here. Real black ice!"

"Are we going to skate on the river?" Amanda asked. "Isn't that awfully dangerous?"

"I looked at it, I tell you," Joe said brusquely. "Of course it's not dangerous. It's a little broken near the shore, that's all. The way it always is."

Looking at her husband's eager, impatient face, Amanda felt a tiny, urgent moment of panic. "Do you think we ought to, Joe?" she went on. "Will there be others out there? Isn't it supposed to be risky alone on a river?" She paused, choking back her nervous, adult's importunacies, suddenly aware that all three Scullins had their eyes on her. They were watching her sharply — three thin, bright-eyed young foxes. Quickly she stood up, grinned back at them, and said, "Oh, all right. It'll be fun. But you'll have to find me *dozens* of extra sweaters, darling." She put her arm around her husband as he went out into the hall. "I haven't seen you all morning," she said.

Joe went out onto the ice first. He had carried three long boards down from the house, and now he laid them, one after another, on top of the heaped white floes of broken ice close to the shore, forming a narrow fifty-foot path from the frozen beach out to the solid ice. "C'mon," he said to Amanda. "It's easy." Bundled to the chin in mufflers and mittens, wearing an old olive-drab Army sweater of his, Amanda followed him, carefully balancing on the unsteady boards, her eyes fixed on the tilted, treacherous slabs beneath her. Out on the ice, she sat on the end of the last board while Joe, whistling cheerfully, laced up her skates. They were alone on the river, and out here, in the middle of the great plain of gray, rumbling cold, Amanda could feel the long sweep of the cruel wind. The small houses on the hill seemed distant and unwatching, and Amanda felt that she and Joe had become two tiny, unnoticed figures under the dark and eyeless sky. After Joe had taken care of Amanda, he laced his own skates and stood up, pulling on his gloves. "Here we go!" he said, grinning and holding out his hands to her. Amanda got up, lurched once, and grabbed at him, and they started off.

It was surprisingly easy at first. Arms crossed, keeping

step, they glided off across the rough ice, moving parallel
with the shore. The wind pushed at their backs, and Amanda
was exhilarated by a feeling of speed and adventurousness,
by her closeness to her husband. Joe guided them expertly,
leading them around occasional triangular heaps of broken
ice that looked like small white campfires. "What are those
things?" Amanda asked.

"Air holes. You just have to be careful to skate around
them. Goodness, Mandy, haven't you ever skated on a river
before?"

"No," said Amanda breathlessly. "I told you I was a home-
body. *Look!* The ice makes waves in front of us."

"Sure it does. That doesn't mean anything. Gee, I wish
I'd thought to bring something for a sail. This wind is
terrific."

But it was too cold to talk, and they went on in a silence
broken only by the scrape of their skates and the occasional
deep booming of the ice around them. Amanda felt the first
sharp aching in her ankles. Already her nose and ears were
numb, and she wished they would turn and start back. Then
she stumbled on a rough spot and almost pulled them both
down, and they stopped. Smiling apologetically, she found
a handkerchief and blew her nose while Joe skated backward in circles around her. She dropped one of her mittens
and then fell down while trying to pick it up. "Look," she
said when she was up again. "You go ahead, darling. I've got
to get back to the boards and sit down for a minute. My
silly ankles are killing me. You can come back in a minute
and we'll skate some more."

"O.K.," he said at once. "Sure you're all right? I'll be

around. You'll get used to it in a while. You're doing fine."
He waved gaily and set off away from the shore, moving
fast, with long, sweeping strides, his hands behind his back.
Smiling grimly, Amanda started back. It was much slower
skating alone, and she moved awkwardly, her body hunched
forward. The rippled ice was terribly rough under her feet,
and the wind in her face filled her eyes with cold tears. Now,
in the gathering winter dusk, the cracking explosions of ice
seemed to come from all around her. She began to shiver
with cold, in spite of her movement. She fell, skated a few
more feet, and then fell again, this time banging her knee
painfully. When she got up again, she looked around for
Joe. For a moment, she couldn't see him at all, and then,
with a lurch of fear, she spied him a great distance off. He
was still moving fast and still skating away from the shore,
a bent, almost invisible figure. He looked to be no more
than a few yards from the line where the ice ended, and
was skating directly for the dark body of choppy open
water in the middle of the river.

"Joe!" Amanda shouted in terror. "Joe! Joe! Come back!"
She waved her arms and called again, but the wind whipped
her thin cries away. She started forward, stumbling toward
him across the expanse of ice, weeping now as she called,
"Joe! Come back, Joe! Oh, please! Oh, *please* come back!"
But the tiny figure went on, looking like a small child in
the distance as it moved ever closer to the edge of the water.
Calling and gesticulating, Amanda scrambled along, keeping
her eyes on her husband. Then, before she had time to check
herself, she heard the crash of ice around her and sensed the
sudden, awful failure beneath her feet. She reached for

nothing, cried out again, and then felt the shocking blow of the water.

Later, after Joe had carried her up to the house and after they had stripped off her clothes and rubbed her with towels and dressed her again, in flannel shirts and woollen pants and more sweaters and socks, she lay silent on the couch in the little study, with her arms at her sides and a blanket tucked about her. They found an electric heater and plugged it in beside her, and hurried about, bringing coffee and brandy, smiling at her. But she was cold — cold to the depths of her being. No longer shivering, no longer crying, no longer trying to smile back, she knew now that the real chill was not in her body, not even in her toes. She had been injured more deeply: it was as if a splinter of ice, a fragment of winter itself, had pierced her heart, and she could not speak. Numbly, she watched them while they moved about, three tall strangers talking together, bumping into each other, reassuring each other, already beginning to laugh together while they told her that nothing had happened really — that she had simply fallen through an air hole, and that the river there was only three or four feet deep. She would be warm, they said, in a moment. But she could not respond. She lay there as if in a camp of enemies, wisely holding her tongue. Only her eyes were alive, watching for new perils. When Mr. Scullin poured the brandy into her cup of coffee, she noticed, for the first time, that the first joint on the middle finger of his left hand was missing. She watched while Mrs. Scullin, picking up the disordered room, dumped an ashtray full of cigarette butts into a paper-filled straw wastebasket. Carefully, Amanda stored away these new items of vital intelligence as she lay stiffly on the couch. Mrs. Scullin finally sent the men out of the room, turned off all the lights but one, and sat down across the room from her with some knitting. Trembling lightly from time to time, Amanda lay still in the still room, watching the orange glow of the heater.

She must have slept at last, for she suddenly realized that she had been dreaming. She had been swimming, off some bright and unfamiliar shore, with her husband. For a while he had been with her, smiling beside her in the water, but then she had realized that he had moved far ahead of her and was calling back to her. "Hurry up!" he had called in an excited voice. "Come on out here! It's wonderful out here! You're falling behind." And he had waved to her from the distance, scattering shining drops of water, while she floundered heavily in a dark, cold sea. After she awoke, Amanda was not sure where she was, and she struggled for a moment on the couch against the unfamiliar weight of the strange clothes that bound her. Then she remembered why the blanket was there, and saw the bright coal of a cigarette across the room, where her mother-in-law was sitting. She could hear her husband moving about in the hall outside the study and softly humming to himself.

Then, without any warning, she was crying. She wept silently and heavily, shivering again and choking on her tears as she cried for pity for herself, for her fear, for her remembered dream, and for the lost wife named Rosemary.

Mrs. Scullin limped quickly across the room and sat on the couch beside her. "Child! Child!" she said softly, putting her arms around Amanda. "You're all right now. You're safe now." But Amanda could not stop. The tears came harder, and she turned her head away from the old woman next to her.

"You're *all right*, Amanda," Mrs. Scullin repeated. She smiled at Amanda and lapsed into her normal, rambling conversational voice, her charming, dovelike murmurings about family and family doings. "Why, Joey's right out in the hall, dear. He's cleaning up those paint spots around the bookcase. And Lewis is seeing to the supper, like a dear. Though the good Lord only *knows* what he'll invent. In a minute, we'll all have a nice drink and some supper. We're all here, dear. You're quite safe now. Why, Joey says you weren't *really* in any danger. He says —"

"Stop! Stop!" Amanda burst out at last, jerking herself upright on the couch. "Now you listen to *me!*" She grasped her mother-in-law by the arms and put her swollen, tear-wet face close to hers. "*You tell me what I want to know*," she whispered violently. "Tell me what's wrong with all of you. Tell me about the gun. Tell me about Rosemary. How did your husband lose his finger? How did he get that scar? *Why* didn't Joe take care of Rosemary? What really happened to her — to poor Rosemary? Oh, why did Joe leave me out there today? Why did you break your toe? What kind of crazy people are you, anyway?" She was almost shouting. Then she stopped abruptly, looking sharply to one side. "What's *that*?" she said in a new, choked tone.

"What's what, dear?" Mrs. Scullin said, looking at her anxiously.

"*What's that smell*?" she almost screamed.

"Why, that's only Joey," Mrs. Scullin said in a relieved voice. "I *told* you he was wiping those paint spots up in the hall here. You see, the boys ran out of turpentine this morning, so Joey went out just now and siphoned some gasoline out of the car to use on the paint. He said it's just as good as . . ."

But this time she stopped talking of her own accord as she saw the expression on Amanda's face. Then Mrs. Scullin, too, looked at the cigarette in her hand and beyond it, to the heater glowing on the floor. The two women sat stiffly on the couch, listening, and then slowly looked around as Joe came into the room with a troubled, questioning expression on his young face and the wet rags in one hand.

Côte d'Azur

"I'LL bet he didn't leave a will at all. Probably it'll turn out to be nothing but a charming letter. Or maybe an autographed picture of himself."

The speaker is my sister. She is sitting next to me in the club car of a northbound Pennsylvania Railroad train. In our right hands we each hold a Scotch highball, very strong, the way the railroads serve them, and the ice clinks in our glasses with the rocking and swaying of the car. Outside the big windows opposite us, a hot June day is beginning to cool and fade. The New Jersey back yards that flash by offer up a thousand *Saturday Evening Post* covers. A housewife opens her kitchen door and puts down a dish of dog food. She is whisked away and replaced by three couples in lawn chairs, drinking beer. The women look pretty, for they are wearing shorts, and in front of the group there is a brick barbecue pit with a curl of thin smoke rising from it. Next come three boys playing catch; there is a wild throw and one of the boys leaps for the ball, but before I can see whether he catches it they are gone and I discover a forest of low metal trees ranged before a giant white box

— a drive-in theater. It is too early for the first customers there, but they are expected; the lights are on in the booths by the entrance gate, and two ticket venders — young girls in visored military caps — have moved their stools out into the driveway, where they sit side by side, smiling and waving at us. It is the present streaming by out there — faces, windows, gestures, cars stopped at crossings, trees heavy with new leaves — a landscape without history or meaning. but alive for an instant before us in the long light of early evening.

Inside the train, it is the past. It has been years since I have sat in a club car, and nothing has changed. Down the faded carpet of the center aisle comes the Negro attendant, a courtly smile on his old face, his knees bent against the motion of the train. He snaps a switch at the far end of the car, and the lights come on. The lamp on the wall behind my sister's head is covered with a mosaic shade made of sections of leaded green glass. She and I are in the past, too — much as we hate it — for we are traveling back from Wilmington, Delaware, where we have just buried our father.

Maude is watching me over her glass. She is elegant company. Thin, rather tall, with good legs and a straight back, she is a handsome, citified woman of thirty-eight. She has been a divorcee for eleven years, and she works on fashion accounts in a big New York advertising agency. Her reddish-brown hair is cut short, in a mass of soft curls, and no one looking at her now would guess that her expensive, slender black dress with the single gold pin in the collar, her short white gloves, and her narrow, stylish shoes constitute mourning. Only her eyes look weary. She is three years older than I, and I realize that I am a little afraid of her.

"What do you think, Chris?" she says, with a small, knowing smile. "What do you suppose he left us? Two dozen golf balls for you? Fifty shares of stock in a played-out gold mine for me? Or maybe some unpaid chits from the bar of some first-rate club in Florida. This is an important time for us; we've come into our inheritance."

"Oh, I don't know, Maude," I say, waving my hand. "I don't see why you have to talk like this. I didn't expect anything from him."

"You never expect anything from people, do you, Chris?"

"Oh, are we going to talk about *me* now?"

"No — not unless you want to." She smiles at me again, more gently this time. "But we should have something to say to each other, shouldn't we? Having lost our esteemed sire. But I don't care. I know what I'm going to do. I'm going to ask you to order me another drink."

I must explain that this nervous, unhappy talk is not usual between Maude and me. We are fond of each other, even though we don't show it. We see each other perhaps ten times a year. She always comes to our house in Dobbs Ferry on Christmas Day; the gifts she brings for Louisa and me and our three children are expensive and beautifully wrapped and, without fail, exactly right — the kind of present that instantly astonishes and delights. I am a trout fisherman, and two years ago she gave me a fantastically light bamboo rod that had been handmade in Chile. She comes to visit us for one or two weekends in the summer, and she and I have lunch together in town every few weeks. Perhaps once a year, Louisa and I take her to the theater with us. I was proud of Maude when she won a part-scholarship at Mount Holyoke; I grieved over her short, miserable marriage. I am still proud of her, and perhaps I still regard her just as I did when we were children and her greater age and wisdom awed me. I love Maude, for she is my sister, and families must stay together, but we have little to say to each other. When we have lunch, she relates two or three amusing stories about her office, and asks about the children; I tell her our plans for the summer; we discuss books and plays. We stick to the present, two admiring strangers.

Funerals are grotesque enough when they are on safe home grounds — the commonplace, respectable affair in a church, with the widow looking too controlled, the grandchildren curious and a little frightened, the crazy old female cousin from Virginia who turns up in a back pew even though no one has remembered to write her, and afterward, the friends being determinedly convivial over the highballs and plates of sliced turkey. What Maude and I shared in Wilmington was worse — certainly bad enough to make us snap at each other on the train going home. Our father had died on a Tuesday morning, in the locker room of a country club just outside Wilmington; it was a quick, final stroke. I knew nothing about it until after eleven that night, for it had taken that long for them to find the name and address of a relative. Maude and I went down on the train together Wednesday morning, and the funeral — if you could call it that — was the next day. My wife wanted to come with us, but I didn't know what we would find when we got there, so I told her not to come. On the train going down, Maude and I agreed that he should be buried right there in Wilmington, though neither of us had ever been in that city. There was no other place that made sense to take him. Our mother died in 1954, and, anyway, they had been divorced for years. I hadn't seen him myself for more than two years before he died.

In Wilmington, we went to our hotel and then to the funeral parlor, where, in time, we were joined by a Mr. Summersby, the business associate of my father's who had telephoned me the night before. He was a pale, apologetic man in a shimmering cocoa-colored suit and two-toned loafers. "Honored, honored," he said when I introduced him to Maude. "Though grieved to meet, Ma'am, with things the way they are. This is a terrible thing. A terrible, terrible thing." He looked anxiously back and forth at Maude and me, as if he feared that one of us might begin to cry or ask him whether our father had had any last words for us.

The funeral director's office was air-conditioned, but the day was so heavy that his neat, shiny desk sweated between us while we discussed the endless arrangements and I signed certificates and contracts. In the end, I had to bargain the man down four hundred dollars on the price of a coffin. When Maude and I and Mr. Summersby emerged on the street at two in the afternoon, the sun hit us like a fist.

"I'd be proud to have you to lunch at the club," Summersby said, gesturing toward a large pale-blue convertible. "As my guests, you understand. It'll be cooler there, I can promise you."

A peculiar suspicion began to grow in me when we came in sight of a golf course, some ten miles outside the city. Summersby swung between two white gateposts and drove up a winding driveway, past fairways and old trees and shining greens, to the big stone clubhouse on the top of a rise. I was right; he was taking us to see where our father had died. In the high, shadowy front hall, with its glass-enclosed silver trophies and carved rosters of club champions, Summersby removed his coconut-straw hat and held it in the vicinity of his heart. "It was in there," he whispered to us, nodding toward a door.

"But my God!" Maude cried, turning on him. "Do you think we want to inspect the scene, or something?"

"No, no, no," Summersby said agitatedly. "Of course not. Quite understand. I just thought maybe you'd like to visit his room."

Maude and I looked at each other. "His room?" I said to Summersby. "I don't understand. You mean there's a room here where he sometimes spent the night?"

"Spent the night?" Summersby said, equally confused. "But he *lived* here."

"He lived in a golf club?" Maude said. She turned to me, shrugging and starting to grin. "Maybe he was the caddie master."

"Oh, no!" said Summersby indignantly. "I thought you knew. He was the assistant manager. He was my right-hand man — I'm the manager. I don't know what we're going to do without him. How can I replace him? He was a gentleman through and through."

That night, while Maude and I sat in her bedroom in the

hotel and had a nightcap together, she began to laugh angrily. "Assistant manager of a golf club!" she said, snorting. "Mr. Pieface's right-hand man! Oh, God, Chris, isn't it all just too perfect? The dashing end of our dashing Papa. We should bury him in the eighth bunker, or something. What did you think he did for a living?"

"I don't know," I said uncomfortably. "Estate management — that was what I always thought. That's what he wrote me when he moved here from Phoenix last year. He said it was the same work he'd been in out there but that this was a bigger company. But I thought — you know — an office, and looking after people's money. That sort of thing."

"Me, too," she said. "It all depends what you call it. No wonder he was always so tan."

"I still don't understand it all. I used to write him once in a while, and his address was here in the city. Some company —"

"A letter drop," she said. "He had his mail sent to some friend of his, I suppose. He didn't want us to know. But don't you see that it's *funny*?"

"No, I guess I don't."

"Poor Chris," she said, pulling back her negligee and holding one bare leg out toward the stream of cool air from the air-conditioner. "Poor baby. Do you know that while you and that man went up to see his room, the golf pro came into the dining room and introduced himself to me? His name is Verrazano, or something. He wanted me to know how much they'd all miss Daddy. He said he was coming to the funeral tomorrow. 'That Mr. Drexler was a sport,' he kept saying. 'A real sporting gentleman. All the members liked him so much. He was what you'd call a likable man.' He gave me the idea somehow that playing golf was part of Daddy's job — that he was always on tap to help make up a foursome, or whatever you call them. He said, 'You know, Miss, your father shot a seventy-eight just last Friday. Sixty-three years old and he shoots a seventy-eight.' He wanted me to be proud of that. Is seventy-eight good, Chris?"

"Yes, it's good," I said.

"What was his room like?"

"Oh, nothing much. What you might expect."

My father's room was over the caddie shop. There had been one business suit in the closet, and fifteen or twenty sports jackets and pairs of slacks. There was a narrow bed, a dresser with a half-empty bottle of bourbon on it, a small bookcase, a desk, and one worn easy chair. Nothing more. I had gone through the desk drawers quickly. There was a checkbook from a local bank, showing a balance of two hundred and eighty-four dollars, a copy of the club regulations, some letters from a woman in Santa Barbara, and more letters, which I did not open, postmarked from places like Mexico City and Miami and Cannes. In the back of one drawer I found a loose heap of photographs, including several snapshots of my children that I had sent him over the years. There was a faded photograph of me and Maude and a donkey, taken in France in the summer of 1933, and this I put into my pocket. Before I left the room, I glanced at the fifteen or twenty books in the shelves. One of them looked older than the others, and I took it out. It was *The Ordeal of*

Richard Feverel, and the bookplate inside said "Williams College Library." My father had gone to Williams. The slip in the back showed that the book had been overdue since May 3, 1919.

It was dark by the time our train entered the tunnel that leads under the river. I took out my commuting timetable and began to estimate how long it would take me to get across town to Grand Central. But then under Penn Station, when we were waiting with the other passengers in the little hall at the end of our Pullman car and the train was creaking slowly along the platform, Maude turned to me and said, "Chris, would you mind horribly seeing me home?"

"No," I said, surprised. "I was just going to put you in a cab, or have you drop me at Grand Central. But I'll take you home."

"You can catch a later train, can't you?" The porter opened the door, admitting a cloud of damp, fetid air upon us, and she turned away. "I'm sorry, Chris," she said quietly over her shoulder. "It's silly of me. It's just that today has been — And I never see you."

"No, it's fine," I said. "Perfectly fine. I can get a train any time." I had been selfish, trying to rush off like that.

Maude lives in a dingy, comfortable old apartment house in the East Sixties, near the river. When we got there, I paid off the cabby and carried our two suitcases in. In her apartment, Maude went around turning on lamps, opening windows, and drawing the curtains. "It'll be cooler in a minute," she said. "I always get a breeze up here, and that's nicer than the air-conditioner."

I looked at my watch. "Look, Maude," I said. "It's silly for me to try to get home tonight. It's after nine, and I'd just have to turn right around and come back again in the morning. Louisa won't mind. Why don't you let me take you to dinner somewhere, and then I'll check into a hotel for the night?"

"Oh, Chris, it would be wonderful," she said. "But I won't have you staying in a hotel. You can sleep right here in the living room. That couch makes a bed, of sorts. And we can eat here. I'm sick of restaurants. I'm sure I can rustle up something for us. Let's have a cocktail, and then you can call Louisa."

Sitting on the edge of Maude's bed and sipping a Martini, I talked to my wife. Her voice, low and concerned for me, made me wish I were at home. I could see her sitting by the telephone table in the hall, with the front door open and the smell of the summer night all through the house. Then my sons talked to me, one after the other, and told me the score of the ball game they were watching, and then my fourteen-year-old daughter, Eliza. She sounded preoccupied and upset. "Is anything the matter?" I asked, suddenly anxious.

"No, but tomorrow's my history final and I've *got* to keep studying. I just can't waste any more time gossiping like this."

I laughed and wished her luck, and hung up.

I found Maude in the kitchen, stirring something in a bowl. "I'm going to make you a fabulous soufflé," she said. "I *hope*. That and a salad. And I found a bottle of white wine on the ice. We'll have a party, Chris."

She was barefooted and she had tied an apron around her

waist. She suddenly looked very young, and I realized that she must be lonely a great deal of the time. I thought of her cooking in the evenings like this, alone in the neat, silent apartment. "Do you always cook for yourself, Maude?" I asked.

"Sure," she said, bending to light the oven. "I'm a master of heat-and-serve. I'm famous for my instant chow mein."

"You should get married, Maude."

"Fat chance," she said. "I wouldn't be any good at it. And besides, there aren't any men." She glanced at me almost angrily. "Don't get soft about me, Chris," she said. "I get along."

Our dinner did seem almost like a party. Relieved of the solemnities and degrading surprises of the past two days — the handful of perspiring strangers at the cemetery, and the man who had taken me aside after the ceremony, stammering with embarrassment, to present me with a small bill of my father's from a local tailoring and dry-cleaning establishment — Maude and I sat opposite each other at a little table in her living room, with the lights turned out and candles flickering between us in the warm breeze from the window. We could hear the cries of boats on the East River. We stayed there after our coffee and slowly finished the bottle of wine. We laughed and yawned, and, for once, we talked about our childhood. We tried to remember the names of the long succession of cleaning women and part-time maids who had worked for my mother through the years when the

three of us had lived in a small apartment on Riverside
Drive.

"And then there was — oh, *God,* what was her name,
Chris?" Maude said, her face alive with warm candlelight.
"The one who came just after Christmas that year? It was
the time when I was sick in bed with the ear abscess. She was
Irish, and she quit the day you brought me that garter snake
from school. What *was* her name?"

"I don't know," I said. "I can't remember."

"Oh, you know, Chris. Remember, she found the snake in
the Slaters' shoebox in the bathroom, where you'd left it,
and she came out screeching? *Lily!* — that was it. Lily
O'Something." She began to laugh. " 'Oh, Jesus, a ser-pint!'
she yelled, and she ran right out of the house. You made me
promise not to tell Mummy."

The telephone rang, and Maude went off to the bedroom
to answer it. She was gone a long time. I cleared the dishes
and stacked them in the sink, and then I stood by the window and smoked and stared down into the street. Then I
remembered the snapshot I had found in my father's desk
and I went to my jacket, hanging on the back of my chair,
and took it out of the pocket. In the picture, Maude is about
eleven years old. She has thick hair that falls just to her
shoulders, her arms and legs are tan and thin, and her cotton
dress looks too small for her. She faces the camera with a
small, grave smile, but the photograph has faded and it is impossible to see the expression in her eyes. I stand beside her,
my head reaching the level of her chin, and the donkey is between us, his long, foolish face peering over our shoulders

and his ears forming the apex of the composition. My right hand is caressing his nose. I am wearing a striped jersey, abbreviated shorts, and sandals. There is a bandage on my knee, where I had cut myself on the rocks at the *plage*, and eventually, I remember, the cut became infected and had to be opened by a doctor in Nice. Looking at the snapshot that night, I found that I could not recall the name of the donkey, or even remember who had taken the snapshot. All I could add to the picture was the look in Maude's eyes. Her eyes had been large and very dark, with deep, winglike shadows beneath them; she had watched the world with a solemn, unblinking stare. Those eyes had frightened me, for that summer I believed that they saw more than mine did — down corridors at night, through closed doors, through lies, and through the false smiles of adults who are talking to children.

Maude came back into the living room and sat down. "Sorry," she said. "A friend. He wanted to console me on our great loss. I told him you were here."

"He can come up, Maude," I said, feeling in the way. "I don't mind at all."

"As a matter of fact, he *can't* come up," she said. "He's married." She shrugged. "Another hopeless cause. What do you have there?"

I handed her the photograph and told her where I had found it. She drew in her breath and then turned on the lamp beside the sofa and held the picture in the light. "That was the summer it all happened," she said. "This was just after Daddy went off. It's you and me and Beppo."

"I couldn't remember his name," I said.

"I guess you were too young to remember much. His name was Beppo. He lived right next door to the Cossarts. I doted on him."

"Maude," I said, sitting down beside her, "why did Father leave that summer? I asked Mother a couple of times, but she never said. Why did he go off like that?"

"He didn't love us enough," she said.

"What?" I said. I was startled.

"He didn't love us enough," she repeated loudly.

"Oh, come on, Maude," I said. "That's no kind of answer. I mean, where did he go when he disappeared like that?" I was annoyed; I had a feeling she was putting me off.

"Oh, who *cares?*" she cried. "He didn't love us enough. That's the only answer. It's just like you to want an explanation, Chris."

"What does that mean?"

"Oh, I know you! You just want to understand him. You want all the facts and then you think you'll know what kind of a man he was. You're so damned understanding, Chris. You're so safe."

"I see," I said curtly.

"Oh, Chris, .just look at yourself!" she said, the words bursting out of her. There were tears in her eyes. "You *are* safe, you poor baby. You're thirty-three or thirty-four years old, and you're an old man. You might as well be sixty. You've got everything — a nice, safe house in the country, safe wife, safe children, a safe, fat job. Chris, what are you *doing* as assistant regional almighty Pooh-Bah in a tools company, anyway? You could have done better for yourself. You could have been anything, Chris — anything in the world — and just look at yourself. Me, I'm not bright enough and I don't care enough about the damned career thing to do more than the silly work I do, but you, Chris — you're a man!"

"Why don't you just stop about me?" I said. I was shaking.

"All right, I'll stop. I'll stop in a minute, dear Chris. Dear brother that I love." She put her hand on my arm. "But damn it, just once — just this one time — *look* at yourself. Why didn't you go away to college, like everybody else, instead of living at home with Mummy and just going to Columbia? Why did you get married when you were twenty? Why did you have a baby right away?"

"I was in love," I said. "But maybe you don't know about that."

"All *right!* Maybe I had that coming. But Chris, look at the way you live! Look at those silly friends of yours at home. I know — I've met them. Those golfers, those bridge players. Those plump wives at dinner parties all talking to each other instead of to the men. What are you doing in a place like that, you poor booby? Have you ever once taken a chance — had a real love affair, punched somebody in the nose, gotten drunk for three days? Don't you think maybe you've missed something? Didn't you ever want to run away to sea?"

"*Now* I get it," I said. "You want me to be like Father. Is that it?"

She looked at me and then she gave an angry little laugh and wiped the tears from her face with the back of one hand. "Just listen to us," she said. "What cheap talk." She got up and found a handkerchief in her pocketbook and blew her nose. "Now I *have* stopped," she said. "Try to forgive me. I don't know — maybe I'm a bit drunk."

She went out, and I could hear the water running in the bathroom. When she came back, she was wearing a bathrobe and carrying some clean sheets over her arm. She had taken off her makeup. "Help me fix up your bed, Chris," she said. "I think we're both done in. And no wonder."

We pulled the couch away from the wall and tucked the sheets about it. She found me a clean towel and facecloth and took the candles and tablecloth away. I kissed her good night, and then, just as she was going into her bedroom, I remembered something. "Maude," I said, "why didn't you go up to see his room yesterday?"

"I don't know," she said. "I just didn't want to, somehow." She paused for a moment in the door. "You don't remember him, do you, Chris?" she asked in a low voice.

"Sure I do," I answered. "He used to turn up every few years and we'd have lunch. You remember how he was. He even came out to the house once or twice. And before that, years ago, when we were in school, the way he'd suddenly appear sometimes. He took us to the Music Hall once."

"I don't mean that," she said. "I mean before, when he was still at home."

"I guess I don't really remember. I can remember him teaching me to swim. That sort of thing."

"Do you remember him reading aloud?"

"No."

"He read wonderfully. He could make you see everybody in the book. . . . There was no way of knowing he was going to turn out the way he did."

Long after Maude had closed her door that night, I was still kicking at the sheets that clung to my sweating legs and turning from one side to the other on the narrow, unfamiliar couch. Finally, I got up and took off my rumpled pajama top and then pulled the bottom sheet smooth and tucked it in again. I found a cigarette and an ashtray, and got back into bed. I lay on my back and smoked and stared at the lights moving across the ceiling. Sounds of cars, fragments of talk, and the tap of late walkers' heels on the sidewalk drifted into the room from the street, and once there was a man's voice, absolutely distinct, crying "Connie! Connie! Connie!" in terrible distress. Lying there with the noise of the city in my ears, I had a frightening moment of clarity when I thought I could understand why Maude and I had never wanted to talk about our common history. It seemed to me that we were like two survivors of a sudden, devastating air raid that had struck one morning when we were in different parts of the same town. We shared the experience, but meeting later we would find that neither of us was able to understand what the other had seen and felt, so violent was the memory of our own, private disaster. She would try to tell me about the bomb that had landed on the fish store just down the street, blowing the glass from her front windows all over her at the moment when she was down on her hands and knees taking up the hem of her old green dress. And I would interrupt her: "Yes, yes, but *I* was in a barbershop when they hit the grammar school on the corner, and the power lines came down all over the street. I had to walk out through the smoke, and there were loose schoolbooks lying in the stones and dirt, and I never did get home that day."

Then, for the first time in many years, I turned myself back to France and the summer of 1933. I started with the photograph, but nothing came; I could not remember the donkey. Instead, I caught sight of a long, slope-nosed, shiny black Renault car, with my father at the wheel. He was wearing tweeds, and the four of us were driving south from Paris. We stopped in Grasse (I could see the shape of the little wooden vials of solid perfume they gave Maude and me at one of the factories), and then — instantly, in my recollection — we were at Saint-Caylus, a small fishing-village resort on the Riviera, and we had come unstuck. I cannot remember my father leaving; he was simply gone, and then, within a day or two, my mother was gone, too, taking the car, and Maude and I were left with the Cossarts. Our mother must have got their name through the hotel; almost certainly they weren't known to her until the day she realized that she had to place her children somewhere while she went off in pursuit of her husband. Perhaps she wasn't pursuing him, but why would she have left us otherwise?

I can remember the Cossarts' garden better than the house itself. There was a high wall of flaking gray stone around both the house and garden, topped all along its length by a narrow roof of tilted red tiles. Sometimes, on hot mornings, a sliver of wall would appear to come alive for an instant as a slim lizard, exactly the color of the stone, would leap for an insect. When I approached, keeping my eye on the spot, the lizard remained invisible until I had crept close enough to detect his tiny shadow pencilled on the wall beneath his pulsating ribs. He would swivel one slitted eye toward me, watching my descending hand, and then dart away, sometimes leaving the tip of his tail between my thumb and forefinger.

Mme. Cossart is only a shape to me. She has no face in my recollection, but she is tall and rather forbidding and, like so many middle-aged French women, dressed entirely in black. She might have been in mourning. I know she was French — that was why we called her Madame. But Mr. Cossart was English. We called him Herbert, and he is easier for me to visualize. He is small and red-faced, with white hair combed straight across the top of his head; his shirtsleeves are rolled up and there is a small, blurred purple tattoo — a bird, perhaps — on the inside of one forearm. I can only think of the Cossarts separately — never as a couple. Herbert would announce at breakfast that the four of us would rent a car that afternoon and drive to Nice for haircuts and ice cream; Mme. Cossart would look at him with pitying distaste and say that, *au contraire*, we would stay at home, for it was surely going to rain. Madame would pour a half glass of wine for Maude at dinner, and when Herbert protested and said that what we wanted was a glass of good fresh milk, Madame would go wordlessly to the cupboard and fetch another glass and fill it with wine for me. It seems likely that my mother hired the Cossarts because they were the only couple she could find at Saint-Caylus who could speak English to Maude and me and were willing to take us in. I think

Herbert and Madame spoke French to each other, but I am not certain, for I cannot remember a single conversation between them. Where had they met and married? Why did they live in an obscure French village beside the Mediterranean? What did our mother tell them of our circumstances and needs? I shall never know.

Every afternoon after lunch, in the hottest part of the day, Madame made me lie down on a cot for a full hour's nap on a small ground-floor porch at the back of the house. I insisted that at eight I was too old for naps, but Madame said that children could not have too much sleep. I didn't sleep, of course; stripped to my underwear and dazed with heat, I would lie there waiting endlessly for the bell on the alarm clock in the kitchen to ring and terminate my sentence. I could hear the high singing of locusts in the hot garden outside and, more softly, the ceaseless small crashing of waves on the beach, just down at the end of the road. Then, almost every day, the back door would bang and Herbert would appear in the garden, wearing a dirty white Panama hat and carrying garden implements. Rising and then squatting again, whistling softly to himself, he would make a slow circuit of the flowerbeds, leaving a trail of pulled weeds on the brick walk as he worked his way toward me. When he had finished the bed directly beneath me, he would sit down with his back resting against one of the porch pillars, dust the earth off his hands, and produce a wrinkled blue pack of Gauloises. "Well, young Chris," he would say every single time. "Thinking about your papa, I expect."

Sometime early in the summer I must have asked Herbert where my father had gone, for he took it on himself to comfort me and, after his fashion, to explain the matter. Much of the time, of course, I *hadn't* been thinking about my father (I was much more interested in my mother's absence, for instance, or whether there would be another postcard from her tomorrow, or whether we would go to the *plage* that afternoon), but Herbert's obsessive kindness infected me in time, and my father's disappearance became the central fact of my summer.

"Well, now," Herbert would say, blowing a cloud of rich-smelling cigarette smoke into the warm air, "it seems to me that I read in the paper this very morning that they're having a spot of trouble over in Spain these days. Revolutions and that sort of thing. It wouldn't surprise me in the least, young Chris, if that's where your papa has gone. A secret mission for King Alfonso, I should imagine. That will be why he had to pop off like that, unexpected. Secret Service men can never explain their missions, you know. Silent as the tomb, they are. Now, you tell me your papa is a brave man, Chris? Strong? Bit of dash to him? I knew it! Not a shadow of doubt about it; that's where he is — in Spain. He'll be back one of these days. Any morning now, you'll wake up and he'll be here. Perhaps he'll bring a rifle for you and a beautiful lacework shawl for your sister. You mark my words and see."

Every three or four days, Herbert would change his story. My father was in Tripoli, he would say, putting down pirates. He was in Milan, helping distraught Italian bankers to foil a gigantic plot being hatched by a band of cunning safecrackers; he would return with a bag of gold given him for his services. He was in Africa and he would return straight across the sea, with a monkey for me riding on his neck.

Maude was the only one who might have helped me out of this confusion of exciting lies, but Maude belonged to Madame. They were together most of the morning, in the kitchen or walking to the square in Saint-Caylus to shop for groceries, and in the afternoons Madame was teaching Maude to speak French. I was convinced that my sister knew the truth, whatever it was, but I was sure that if I asked her about our father she would look at me coldly out of those great dark eyes and tell me that I was too young to understand, or that Father was dead, or maybe only that I was being *embêtant*.

Once, I must have mentioned the then current version of my father's adventures to Herbert at the dinner table, because I can remember the angry explosion from Madame. "Listen to those two!" she said to Maude. "What stories they tell each other! Now, in truth, Maude *chérie*, I think we have two children in this family and not one of them is wearing skirts. *Quelle histoire!* Now you know what men truly are — inventors and liars and those who run away — and you can be ready for them. Beware of *ces romanciers* — these tellers of bad tales. *Méfiez-vous*."

Our mother came back to see us from time to time. I can remember two visits, and maybe there were more. We would dine with her at the hotel, and once she drove us to Cap d'Antibes for lunch. On those days, Maude became herself again in my eyes — merely my sister — and the hours went by in such a whirl of happiness and excitement that I forgot each time that she would be someone else altogether when we returned to the Cossarts' at night. Mother must have been seeing our father during her absences, or at least hearing from him, because she promised us more than once that he would be back and that the four of us would resume our trip.

Two more events only — the last fragments I can find in me of that long-ago summer. Both are night scenes. In the first, I wake up suddenly, roaring with pain and fright, for a bee has blundered into my bedroom somehow and has stung me under the jaw in my sleep. Herbert is the first one to arrive; he wears a nightshirt and carries an oil lamp in his hand. He examines me, discovers the trouble, and sends Madame back to bed. He goes out and then reappears with a mound of fresh earth from the garden in his hands. He kneels in front of my bed and, to my astonishment, orders me to urinate into the dirt he holds. "Go ahead, Chris," he says sternly, "make water. Do pee-pee. What do you call it?" I protest, but he is adamant, and at last, with some difficulty, I obey. He packs the damp earth into a poultice and immediately claps it on my sting. "Nothing like it, young Chris," he says cheerfully, holding the mud pack on my neck and wiping my tears with the sleeve of his nightshirt. "Draws the sting, draws the hurt."

And then it is the end of the summer and there is a small fête in Saint-Caylus — the celebration of a saint's day. Madame and Herbert take us to the village square that evening, as a treat; we see a strong man in a bathing suit lifting weights, and we eat dinner at an outdoor café to the music of the town band. Afterward, we jam ourselves into a cheerful crowd on a bus that drives us around to the opposite side of the little Saint-Caylus cove, to a beach from which we will have a fine view of the fireworks on the docks. For a long time, we sit on the beach, watching the lights across the cove and waiting for the fireworks. It is very late, long after my bedtime, and I fall asleep there, lying face down in the cool sand with my head in my arms. Some time later, I awake to the sound of cries and applause. Everyone is standing, shouting, pointing. There is clapping and laughter all up and down the beach. Still half asleep, I spring up and look for rockets and fires in the sky. But the fireworks have not yet commenced. Then, following the direction of the pointing fingers all about me, I see what is happening. In the middle of the cove, almost halfway across from the docks, there is a man swimming toward us through the dark water. He swims with one arm held straight above him, and in that hand he carries a lighted flare. Red fire spouts above him, turning the sea to scarlet, and sparks stream over him. The arm he holds aloft is decked with red and blue and white ribbons. The swimmer kicks mightily, sending up showers of spray, and calls to us as he thrashes along. I look at him for an instant and then I go mad with excitement. "It's him!" I cry, rushing toward the water's edge. "It's him and he's come! It's my father, it's my father! He's come for us, he's here!" I run into the warm sea; it covers my sandals and rises to my knees. I turn to the others, pointing and shouting. "Look, Maude!" I call. "Look, Herbert — he's coming! That's my father!"

There is a shocked cry from Madame, and Herbert starts forward, but it is Maude who reaches me first. She runs into the water and seizes my arm and yanks me back so hard that

I fall down. She pulls me up again and then slaps my face. "What's the *matter* with you?" she says between her teeth. "What's happened to you, you little fool? That's not our father! That's just some man." Still holding my arm, she twists me around until her face is right over mine. "Don't you know, Chris?" she says in an angry whisper. "Don't you know Daddy's never coming back?"

Four days later, our mother returns for the last time. She tells us that we will go home without our father. She has sold the car. Herbert accompanies us to the little Saint-Caylus station and sees us off on the local train to Nice, where we will change for the Paris express. A week later, the three of us sail for home on the *Mauretania*.

It was cool the next morning in Maude's apartment, and I awoke feeling rested and eager to get back to my office. I ate my breakfast in the kitchen, while Maude washed our dishes of the night before. She was wearing an old orange cotton bathrobe, but her new makeup and carefully arranged hair gave her a fresh, go-to-work appearance. She put the garbage pail outside the back door, along with the empty wine bottle. "The janitor will think another orgy," she said cheerfully.

I finished a second cup of coffee, and when I had repacked and closed my suitcase, Maude came out of her room wearing a handsome gray silk dress. "You go along, Chris," she said, fastening a bracelet around one wrist. "I'll just pick up your bed and finish up here. You might find a cab on Second Avenue."

We stood by the door, facing each other. She had become the elegant, efficient New York woman, a stranger to me once again. "Are you all right?" I asked.

"Of course I'm all right, Chris. I'm always all right." She gave me a quick hug. "And you're sweet. Look, can you try to forgive me for last night? Those were awful things I said to you and I didn't mean one of them. Just try to remember it as a sudden bout of female hysteria. Because that's what it was. Too much Wilmington. God, how I hate the sticks!"

"Oh, it was nothing," I said. "We were tired. It was my fault, really. I just wanted to find out more about him because — I don't know. I guess I want to be able to remember him the way a son should remember a father."

She took a cigarette from the coffee table and lit it. "Well, you know what there is to remember," she said, shaking out the match. "He was a social director in a gents' club."

"Maude," I said, "you've got to forgive him."

"I'll never forgive him!" she said, her eyes fixed on me. "Never! He was my father. I expect the best from people."

"You could try to love him."

"Oh, Chris," she said wearily. "What do we know about loving people? You've got to let me be myself. You go ahead and love him if you can. You can't make me over, so you'll just have to give up on me."

She picked up my suitcase and handed it to me. "Go along, darling," she said, smiling again. "I'm all right — just Maude. Call me someday next week, and we'll have lunch."

Descending alone in the humming elevator, I suddenly understood my sister. I knew why I had sometimes been afraid of her; her courage was greater than mine. Strong, lovely, self-destructive, bitterly uncompromising, she had loved our father more than I ever could.

Now another train is rolling northward at the end of a summer day. I sit facing forward this time, on a smooth straw seat. I am going home. My suitcase is in the rack over my head, but otherwise everything is as always. My riddled commutation ticket is in the slot in front of me, the corners of held evening newspapers quiver gently to the motion of the train, the tracks make a metallic, slithering murmur under our wheels. Outside, on my left, the Hudson slides by, huge and white and unruffled, reflecting the sun and the empty sky. It fills the middle distance, and by consequence there are fewer figures in this landscape. Several fishermen flash by, sitting motionless on the bank by the roadbed. We overtake two teen-age boys in bathing suits, very tan, riding in a rickety outboard; one of them is sitting on the gunwales up forward, his legs straddling the bow. Then the train slows for a stop, and the land between us and the river widens momentarily, to make room for a dilapidated station, an empty platform, and four empty freight cars on a siding before a small warehouse. The train stops, releasing a few passengers, and then, just as we start forward again, I see a man in an undershirt holding a hose and watering a fenced patch of lawn in front of a grimy one-story wooden house. A yellow dog darts out from behind the house, barking at the train, and is pursued by a young girl in a ponytail. She catches him at the open front gate and seizes him by the collar, holding him until our train goes by. As we pass them, gathering speed, she bends over and says something in the dog's ear, and I find myself smiling.

At this moment, I notice the man sitting next to me, between me and the window. He has put down his newspaper and is staring out with a fixed, sullen expression. His eyes are cold, his smooth cheeks rest puffily on his bulging jaw muscles, and he holds his lower lip between his teeth. He hasn't noticed the house or the girl and the dog; he looks past them and sees a swollen, polluted river concealing corpses.

Uncertain now, I glance about at the other passengers near me. But their expressions tell me nothing; they have hidden themselves behind newspapers and tired private faces. They cannot help me. We cannot compare notes, and none of them has the wisdom to tell me how to live. Each of us has bought his ticket to his own destination and speeds toward it now in his own way — with eagerness, or rage, or despair. There are no victims on this train, no unwilling deportees. The only part of the journey we cannot control is the landscape — the kind of truth we see from our separate windows — and that was arranged for us long before we left the terminal. Bathed in sunlight, our train flies through the late afternoon, rushing for the future.

72
74
75
76
77
79
83
85
89